For the "flash"
efficionado

Happy 27th

Love,

Mom

blink: flash fiction before you can bat an eye

©2006 The Paper Journey Press
The Paper Journey Press
an Imprint of Sojourner Publishing, Inc.
Wake Forest, NC USA

The Paper Journey Press: www.thepaperjourney.com
First trade paperback edition
Manufactured in the United States of America

Library of Congress Control Number: 2006903349

International Standard Book Number (ISBN) 0-9773156-4-9

blink

flash fiction before you can bat an eye

Edited by Wanda Wade Mukherjee

The Paper Journey Press
Wake Forest, NC

To my three boys—Jake, Vik and Kieran —always remember, he who laughs last laughs

blink

Introduction

What's in a name? I asked my arrogant, twenty-something assistant after she informed me that I must choose.

"How can I?' "It's your job," she said. "It's what editors do. Besides, you can't write about every story in your introduction. You've gotta point people in the direction you want them to head like Missouri or Portmanteau."

"Sweet Baby," I replied. "You miss the point. A little bird doesn't just whisper in one's ear. Choosing would be like asking my mother to select a favorite amongst five lovely, but one too many children. I learned a lesson a long time ago that editors may suggest in prefaces, forewords and introductions, for better or worse, what stories readers should read whilst stuck in a breakdown lane or poised at a stoplight, but in the end the reader must read a certain story and weigh for herself whether the author told them something beautiful—cross my heart and hope to die."

"Choose or I quit," was her answer to that soliloquy.

So, on her way to summer's vacation, I commanded she ask Jesus, the clerk at the local SavMore whether, if truly left up to Him, in the end could he—no, would he pick favorites—choose great at being good from those who work hard but sometimes get bogged down in Bedlam with artists rather than poets. What would Jesus do?

Mercy, the consequences I envisioned. What if such choices wreaked retribution in the form of writers peddling shadows or swimming around Long Key just today clothed only in their skin and rain in the middle of a hurricane blinking salt-water tears?

At any rate, this editor would loathe to leave even one writer feeling snubbed. Would they become depressed; stay home, *Inside*, hiding in closets, throwing pink towels at Ivar the Boneless, fearing flashing red lights in distant skies as they rolled down ribbon roads? Would my choices purge them of innocence in the heat of a Spanish summer, cause them to stop dreaming and writing those dreams in wine-stained journals? And what of bats and dogs in our old house abandoned overnight where my own Dad once caught an electric eel in the dead of dark and fried him up for breakfast one Sunday morning on a hot-iron skillet in our backyard Marsh?

"Be good," my lanky, star-struck assistant called from her cell phone. "Choose Rebirth—no midnight hotel lighting."

"I'd rather do an arabesque at night in the country," I retorted, not out of animus for those stories in the particular; on the contrary, I simply disliked having to sit in another sad café waiting for just one bang in my head that might lend me a decision.

Yet I know the readers, the writers, perhaps a critic or two, even my husband expect my opinion so they will know where to start—at the beginning or at the end.

I will be asked, "Which was your favorite story? Your favorite author?" To which I must reply something. Perhaps "these stories meld together in such a way as to question the answer before posing the question; they appear held tightly by some mysterious glue—nocturnal omission—maybe or a mystical reunion of kindred spirits."

"Non sequitur," said my sole's mate.

So here I sit at the end of this ride, a bustle still at the back of my brain. Ready for action, I decide to put pen to paper.

I found Jason Bellipani's protagonist in "Skin and Rain" to be one of the most compelling characters I've come across recently. And, should Kathrine Leone Wright continue to prolifically produce such clean, knotted writing she may well be on her way to being this century's Virginia Woolf— a compliment in the extreme, of course.

Though even I'm aware that in a wink of an eye, for no time at all, anyone will remember I made such a prediction.

— *Wanda Wade Mukherjee*
Wake Forest, North Carolina
2006

blink

Table of Contents

blink

flash fiction before you can bat an eye

Edited by Wanda Wade Mukherjee

The Paper Journey Press
Wake Forest, NC

— Susan Mountain —

Jesus Saves

I parked my shopping cart away from the fish counter so I wouldn't block other shoppers while I browsed. After a few minutes I returned and the basket was gone. Because it was half full of carefully selected produce, the crab and I went in search of my missing basket. After a half-hour of snooping into other shopper's baskets, marching down aisle after aisle, I found the purloined cart abandoned next to the instant Jell-O. An innocent mistake by a fellow shopper gone awry, making me a victim of egregious impoliteness so ordinary as to be annoying in the extreme.

Miffed and disappointed, I finished the rest of my shopping without incident. The checkout line was so long that I read an article on "How to Please Your Man" in *Cosmopolitan*. It suggested doing things that are better left unsaid here. The woman with the big butt in front of me had a cart loaded with two-for-one special turkeys and nothing else. Maybe that's why she seemed so much happier than me.

My astrological forecast in COSMO was replaced by a headline story on the cover of the *National Enquirer*. A photograph of Oprah looking fat and disheveled carried a headline of how Stedman had been unfaithful. But there was no time to ponder this important news. Finally my time had arrived to remove the contents of my cart and place them on the turkey-juice coated conveyer belt.

An unexpectedly pleasant conversation ensued with the check-out guy about the impending Thanksgiving holiday. We talked about the crowds in the store today, my stolen cart, his faraway family, the cost of fresh dill, and all the people who wouldn't be celebrating. His gentle way and kindness soothed me and put me in a better frame of mind. Somehow in the midst of loud, frenzied activity, this clerk just wasn't in a hurry and made time to individualize me.

No longer feeling like an anonymous shopper, I drove home and headed for the fridge and cupboard. With everything stashed away in its proper place, I took a look at my receipt to record the amount in my checkbook. Across the top of under the store number, date, it said, *"Assisting you with a smile—Jesus."* I was stunned.

Had I unwittingly done my shopping in a Christian grocery store? Now I was mad that the store chain had not made this clear to shoppers.

What next? A cross gracing the entryway or a life-sized Jesus cutout beckoning customers to the bread aisle? Someone had to do something. I pulled a piece of stationery from a drawer intent on writing a letter to their corporate headquarters. Suddenly I was struck by the obvious. Proselytizing, other than the acquisition of the almighty dollar, was not part of the store's agenda. Instead of ranting in a letter, I spent the next few minutes laughing out loud.

My checkout guy's name was *Jesus*. A theosophical dilemma of mega proportions, perhaps?

Nope, just Jesus, helping ME save!

Susan Mountain holds a dual degree in Art History/ Photography. She is the digital storyteller of the e-zine *Roshambo*, and has been an exhibiting visual artist for over twenty-five years in the San Francisco Bay Area. Mountain's sense of humor and keen eye for a good story is evidenced in the use of her photograph for our back cover.

blink

— Janet Nodar —
What's In A Name?

"Well, Jasper," said Cynthia. "I guess we're going to be stuck here awhile."

Short brown hair, bleached at the tips, bristled atop Jasper's high, narrow forehead. His square, nerdy glasses had been hip last year, and his skin was the uniform bisque of spray-on tan. He leaned toward her eagerly. She shifted her body on the wooden bar stool so that her breasts were clearly outlined against the fabric of her dress. She kept her glass of bourbon and coke, light on the ice please, and light on the bourbon, in her hand or near it. Cynthia was not a trusting young woman. Rain beat against the sheets of glass that formed the outside wall of the airport lounge. It washed across the acres of concrete, the hangars, the planes. A stroke of lightning split the sky open. The trailing percussion of thunder was so close that for a second Cynthia could feel it vibrating in her chest.

"I would have thought that was a problem a couple of hours ago," said Jasper. "But I don't think I do anymore." He looked into her eyes and smiled. He was probably thirty. He was wearing a sports coat, black polo shirt, khakis. Colored contacts — Cynthia could tell by the flat bright blue of his irises. Jasper was all up for an adventure-filled business trip. He was going to Italy to look at refrigeration units. He worked for a restaurant equipment company. A national chain. So exciting.

"Are you married, Jasper?" said Cynthia.

"No, Jennifer, I'm not. Are you?"

She shook her head. She didn't believe him, but it didn't matter. Cynthia had told him her name was Jennifer. Today, unusually, her plane ticket (to Houston and then on to Buenos Aires) was in her true name. She even had her own passport in her money belt. It was a little unnerving. But nobody seemed to be looking for her. She'd made it through security no problemo. Jasper's expensive-looking laptop case sat on the floor below his leather loafers, which were casually braced on the rungs of his barstool. He wore a Rolex that looked real to Cynthia's careful eye. "Nope," said Jasper, "now I think this storm is just fine. Another round?"

The bartender served them, and slid a keypad toward Jasper. He punched in his debit code again. 548 — and, like before, his hand moved slightly and hid the last digit. No problemo, thought Cynthia. With three, she could figure out the fourth in no time. He kept his flat leather wallet in his sport coat's inner breast pocket. "Let's finish these and go for a walk," she said. "Stretch our legs. Lord knows how long we'll be stuck on our planes."

"Sounds good to me," said Jasper.

The sky split open again, this time the lightning so close it lit up the bar, the bartender's profile, the backdrop of bottles. Cynthia shrieked, her hands at her mouth. The thunder unrolled, and all of the lights in the airport went out. For the merest shimmer of time the world was pitch black, and then generators brought the building back to life. Jasper's left hand was on her back. His right was in his jacket pocket. "You okay? You seemed a little startled."

She stiffened. She did not particularly enjoy it when strangers touched her. He seemed to sense this; his hand fell away from her, and he turned his body toward the bar. She drained her weak bourbon and coke. "Still up for a walk?" she said. He nodded, abandoning his own almost-full glass. He was a brisk walker. The airport's halls seemed endless, a human ant farm, with sproutings of boutiques and cheap food and coffee stands every few yards. They browsed in a dimly lit clothing store. Jasper surprised her by insisting on buying her a soft pale yellow sweater. He paid cash, a fact which interested her less than it normally would have. The sweater was not a color, or a texture, that suited her, but she pretended to be pleased. She was used to men who wanted to dress her some certain way, although she wouldn't have thought that Jasper was that type. Cynthia began to feel unwell. Dizzy. Nauseated. Her head hurt. She wanted to lay down. She could not go any further. Jasper steered her into an empty hallway behind an unlabeled gray door. "You sonofabitch," she said to him, looking directly into his flat blue eyes. But her own insisted on closing. It was as if she blinked, and never unblinked.

It was the cold that woke her, or perhaps it was the pain in her legs and back. She couldn't see anything; the darkness was thick, viscous, as if it had hardened over her eyes. She was lying on a concrete floor. She was naked. She reached out and felt a wall. A corner. Wall. Doorframe. The other way; a janitor's bucket, a stiff mop. She recognized the smell of dirty cleaning water. She was in a closet. She sat up, cautiously, and her head rang with pain. She felt her own breasts, her stomach, her slimy crotch. He'd raped her. Jesus Christ. Her money belt was gone. Her passport, her plane tickets, her cash, her collection of cards. Her clothes. He'd taken her watch off her wrist, taken her earrings. Her suitcases were on their way to South America. Her fingers slid up the wall until she found a light switch.

And she saw that he had left her something, after all. The pale yellow sweater he'd bought her, folded in a neat square. And a note on top, stuck to a debit card. "Don't remember me, do you?" it read. "But I sure remember you, baby. I think you got the first three digits on this card, didn't you? Good luck, Merideth. Jennifer. *Cynthia*."

Janet Nodar is a freelance reporter who writes about business, the shipping industry, and wine. She is married, has two kids, and is working on a novel.

— Tiffany Noonan —

Arabesque

My prince, I'm sorry. I have no excuses. I should have been prepared. *Rond de jambe à terre*—leg extended, toes pointed, arms in fourth position— just for you. Hair and nails perfect, painted. Shaped. But I wasn't. I didn't have the time. The money. I thought I would get a chance to visit the salon before we met again. Look at my ends; they haven't been trimmed in ten years. *Belle-mère* wouldn't let me bring scissors outside the sewing room. She never worried I would hurt myself, but they were just too fine for someone like me. I couldn't afford etiquette books, so I minded the hearth. (I imagined fairies in ember tutus dancing *pas de deux* with fireflies. Such were the dreams of a little girl.) Whenever the logs snapped at me, I knew I'd done something wrong. Now I have snapped. My *belle-mère* has snapped. The glass has snapped. But enough of my chatter. I will take care of everything. That is what I do. If you look away—only for a moment so I may *relevé*—I'll be perfect. Blink, and I will be your *princesse arabesque*. Once you open your eyes, the arch of my foot will be the arch of my spine. You'll see how I can bend for you, just as I bent for my sisters. Don't look down at my feet. No, please. If you must, then at least ignore my calluses. I promise they'll fall off once I don't have to stand on *en pointe* anymore.

Tiffany Noonan's work has appeared in several journals. Her latest project is *four sparks fall*, an experimental novella. She will receive her MFA in fiction from Florida Atlantic University in May 2006.

— Laura Halferty —

Sunday Morning

I t's Sunday morning and you think you might be pregnant.

At the drugstore you head straight for THE AISLE, the one with all the stuff you occasionally have to buy but don't want anyone to see you buying. One test seems as good as the next, so you grab one that's on sale and survey the store to assess your checkout prospects. A kid with dyed black hair and acne is manning one of the front counters, trying to look bored and cool. Back at the pharmacy counter you see a cashier with a scowl on her face listening to an old man preaching on and on about shoddy service.

You decide to take your chances at the pharmacy counter. You don't much feel like handing the test to the boy. It would be like saying, "Hi! I've been having sex!" and you'd rather not play a part in Creepy Drugstore Boy's fantasies.

The woman behind the counter, no doubt still reeling from the old man's sermon, looks at you as you set the test down and says, "Is that it?" And you think, Isn't that enough?

When you get home you open the test and get down to the business of reading the instructions. There are instructions in both Spanish and English, but you prefer the Spanish. Not that you understand them, but the Spanish seems more cheery. The English instructions sound fateful, all Anglo-Saxon doom and gloom.

In the bathroom you hold the stick in your "urine-stream" and count to ten. Then you carefully place the stick on the sink and go into the bedroom to wait. The bedroom clock says 11:03. In three minutes you'll know. You pace around the room and think about the women in all those commercials, so pretty and hopeful, sitting on white couches with supportive husbands holding their well-manicured hands.

At 11:06 you begin moving in the direction of the bathroom.

You approach the sink casually.

You pick up the stick.

You make vows to any god listening: You'll never have sex again, never put yourself in this position again.

But none of that matters right now because your life is still your own.

Laura Halferty teaches writing and literature at the State University of New York at Oswego. Her fiction has been published in *Women Behaving Badly: Feisty Flash Fiction Stories,* and *Feminista!: The Journal of Feminist Construction.*

— Sandra Levy Ceren —

Blind Date

A quarter moon lit his path through the thick oleander shrubs of the condo complex. Confident that this evening would go as well as the others he had so carefully planned, Rick scanned the area, darted between the heavy foliage and stopped to tighten the hood of his black sweat suit.

Rick imagined the young woman emerging from the shower, wrapping a terry-robe around her slender body and dolling herself up for their date. Just like the others, she was in store for a surprise certain to terrify her but to delight him. The anticipation of stifling her screams and turning her joyful expectation into a bloody horror aroused him.

The scent of vanilla wafted from a window, probably from hers. She had invited him for coffee and probably baked in his honor. Set the table with flowers, switched on the stereo, too, as the others had done. How stupid they all were!

Rick grinned as he considered his clever scheme. Choosing vulnerable, unsuspecting targets, his impeccable methods produced for him a package of pleasure wrapped in secrecy. Better than the time he had worked the night shift as a mental health tech in the hospital. No one had suspected his wee-hour marauding where cat-like he had slipped into the beds of female patients.

Recalling those adventures, he had an erection. Not yet,

he told himself. When the hospital cut costs, they discharged him. He felt that peculiar admixture of pleasure from his covert activities and anger at the dismissal. Now, recalling that time, his muscles tensed and his head throbbed.

Sheltered behind the stout trunk of a date palm, Rick poked his head out and saw the woman silhouetted against the window shade. He stepped closer for a better view. A dog barked and another echoed in response. He couldn't calculate the direction of the barking, but he knew she lived alone and had no dog to protect her.

Someone opened a window and flashed a light in his direction. An exciting current charged up his spine as it always did when he faced risk. Quickly, he ducked behind a camellia bush.

The flashlight went off and the window closed.

He waited a few minutes. All was still. He glanced at his Rolex and strolled toward the rendezvous, reassured by the weight of the knife in his pocket

Smiling broadly, she led him into a room scented with freshly brewed coffee. What a fool she was, seemingly unwary of the way he was dressed. When he made the date, he had identified himself as an executive who had attended a conference with her last month. He stepped closer then whipped out his knife. His date screamed.

A policeman crashed out of the closet, pointing a gun at him demanding, "Drop the knife. Raise your hands above your head. Now!"

Rick hadn't known that the woman's brother was the chief investigator working the serial rape case.

Sandra Levy Ceren Ph.D, pens a popular newspaper column *Ask Dr. Ceren*. She has published numerous short stories and two mystery novels *Prescription For Terror* and *Secrets From The Couch*, featuring a psychologist-amateur sleuth.

— Marie Kelly —

Purging Innocence

Everyone comes back to my place after the bar. Most of them have passed out and I decide, now, with the proper amount of liquid courage in me, that it's time to tell Peter how I feel. We've been friends ever since Mark Bennet's seventh grade boy-girl birthday party. I know he has a girlfriend. I know it's impossible for anything to happen. I'm not even sure I want anything to happen because I like that feeling I get in my stomach when I see him. "I need air, wanna go for a walk?" I whisper to him. "Yeah." I put my scarf on and we take off down the sidewalk toward Dame Street. We're walking fast and I can hear the crunch crunch crunch of the leaves beneath our feet. I breathe in deep and smell burning leaves and feel like a kid again. "I have to tell you something," I say and put my hand to his chest, stopping him. "And I don't want you to say anything." "Okay," he says hesitantly. "Not a word, promise?" "Promise." "I have a crush on you." He smiles and we start walking again. I shiver and tug on my coat, squeezing it as tight as I can around my ribcage. We walk all the way down to Dame Street and cross over to the park. I shuffle through the leaves and smile and feel my freezing nose drip a little so I suck it in.

"I'm tired, you wanna sit?" Peter asks. "Sure," I say. "Race ya to the swings!" I take off running and plop down on a cold plastic swing and dangle my feet, tickling the sand below. Peter sits next to me and we swing for a bit, and I've never felt so free, until he stops abruptly. I turn to face him. "Can I tell you something now?" he asks and I nod. "And I don't want you to say anything." "Shoot," I say. "Really, don't say anything, okay?" I raise my right hand and make an X sign over my heart. "My girlfriend had an abortion last week," he says, and looks down at his feet. I stare down at my own feet and feel my liquid courage creep back up. I notice a leaf sticking out of my left shoelace, and purge.

Marie Kelly is currently working on her first novel after running a record label out of Detroit for seven years. She resides in Ferndale, Michigan.

— Jason Bellipani —
Skin and Rain

There is a moment, a flicker, when you suddenly recognize that someone, a person, is an animal—their naked chest, warm and collapsible and so much like clay. You worry that raindrops will leave scars.

I help lower my mother-in-law step by step down the narrow staircase into my basement; the one I'm finishing with a playroom and a workout room and closets that won't click closed. The one I build each day, by myself—the one I will never use because two weeks after my mother-in-law dies this house will go up for sale and we'll move in with her husband of forty years.

The walls brush against my shoulders as we descend; I'm behind her, with my hands secured under her arms, supporting her weight. "That's the best," she says.

Her husband crouches in front, helping to lift each leg and place it on the next step down; he encourages her to keep going. We pause on each stair so she can conjure or re-group or hold herself together—like she'd spill out of her skin if she didn't want to see the basement. Then after a moment, she makes herself solid and stiff again and says "Okay." I lift, glad that I am strong enough to do something about this situation.

At last she arrives at the bottom. A standing lamp illuminates an unpainted room — two rooms — more complete in my imagination than in their physical reality. The white walls are bumpy and peeling with drywall tape that won't stick; the ceiling is low, an inch taller than the top of my head, and made from pieces of stiff white foam with ragged edges that do not meet. The air smells like cut wood and wintergreen tobacco.

The walker unfolds easily and my mother-in-law shuffles in her blue slippers across the cement floor from one room to the other, complimenting my efforts. She says that she's glad to see this, that she needed to see this—but I doubt that.

This mess is not an accomplishment; it is an exercise in make-believe. I sound like a kid trying to explain his fort to grown-ups. When the baby is born, I say, she can play with her brother in this area while I lift weights over here. Toys and books could go in shelves along there or inside here. But my mother-in-law does not roll her eyes or laugh at my tilted closet door; she looks thoughtfully around and nods, as if she sees my imagined version of the basement with a baby girl crawling across a field of red and blue blocks, a blond haired boy playing with two plastic Spidermen.

I notice the large gap in between two pieces of drywall that I had filled and smoothed over with spackle; it has dried and cracked like a patch of desert earth.

Then I stand in front of my mother-in-law my hands gripping under her arms again. "That's the best," she says. I lift her and step up backwards, hunched forward, trying to do it perfectly, trying to make it easy. I've never been this close to her before, so close that I can see too much of her skin—on her neck, her forehead, the small wrinkles around her mouth.

And it's not pleasant.

I wish she was just my mother-in-law on a phone in the future, not here in front of my face, waiting and resting on a step with her eyes closed re-focusing her energy for the climb back up. Her legs are dead weight but I lift her easily, stepping up backward and then pausing, still hunched, still holding her.

Her husband stands above and behind her —silent. In two months he'll help me carry boxes up these stairs and load them into the station wagon. Heavy boxes, filled with pots and books and cartoon books I drew when I was ten. But right now I'm holding his wife of forty years and she's not wincing in pain, her face is not twisted in anguish or desperation—it looks as smooth and beautiful as my pregnant wife's face. For a moment, I imagine she's taking a break on her cross-country skis or standing on the dock at the lake savoring the moment before glides into the water, her lithe body a stream of bright blue.

I stand by the window and watch as he helps her into the station wagon. She sits on the passenger seat and reclines back all the way, until her head and body have disappeared from view; the last thing I see are her finger tips, still and white, pressed against the glass.

Later the baby's white skin will cause me to remember this day. My fingers touch her naked baby's back, my hands under her arms, and I raise her up until her head almost touches the ceiling. She smiles down at me.

And in one instant, one flicker of a breath, I recognize her frail animal body, too tender, and too smooth to ward off anything. I blink, and I know that one day, raindrops will melt this baby away.

Jason Bellipani lives and writes in New Hampshire. His work has appeared in The Cream City Review, The Berkeley Fiction Review, and Sniper Logic.

— Brandy Foster —
Little Bird

The icy cold stung her face and penetrated her thin robe. The fingers on her right hand gripped the gritty concrete surface of the low wall that edged the perimeter of the rooftop garden. She looked out across the wall into the dingy city, taking in the brick façades of the old warehouses, the empty pre-dawn streets. Her husband had talked her into coming here; they used to live an hour from town, an hour from anywhere. Not so long ago, when they'd been invited down here for dinner at a friend's, he was smitten with the converted warehouse condos—with their bare-brick walls, exposed ductwork, and exorbitant price tags—that the city was promoting to revitalize its dying city center. However, she knew that this city was already dead, beyond resuscitation.

A tiny movement to her left caught her eye.

There, not three feet from her, a tiny sparrow had landed on the wall. Like her, it was surveying the city, perhaps trying to determine where to go next.

She resisted the urge to reach toward the little bird; she didn't want to startle it. She didn't want it to fly away.

I mustn't touch it, she thought. It's so tiny and fragile; its poor little heart couldn't take it. I would frighten it to death. No, don't reach for it. Don't be selfish this once. You'll scare it away. Please don't scare it away.

Last year, during her commute from her job in the city,

she would relish her hour to herself. Occasionally, when just the right song came on the radio, she would press the button and the moon roof would glide open. She would crank up the radio to hear it better over the wind.

During those moments, she would envision herself soaring away. It was always the same. She would unbuckle her seatbelt and reach up through the moon roof and grip the car with both hands and lift herself. Then, without slowing down, the car somehow propelled forward, she would gracefully push off from the steering wheel with her toe, like a ballet dancer, and she would soar out into the wind. She liked to think about the astonished faces of the drivers in the cars behind her. How they would marvel to see her soar up into the wind, her trajectory taking her far into the sky, far out of sight, far, far, into oblivion.

Startled by the sudden movement, the little bird took flight.

Brandy Foster lives an hour from anywhere with her fabulous husband and their two precocious children. She teaches Freshman English at Wright State University in Dayton, OH, where she is completing her Master's degree.

— Erin Murphy —

Blinking For Each Moment

All it takes for anything to change is a heartbeat. An instant. In a flicker of an old light-bulb, in one bright moment, everything is perfect —Flash!— It's falling apart. And part of me is screaming that it will never be okay. That I'll always have a broken piece inside me that's crying and crying and crying. Bits of a shattered heart escaping through rainy eyes; it hurts less once it's gone.

The rational part of me says, "It'll be okay. I'll close my eyes tonight and wake up someday, stronger and dancing."

Despite the tears that are falling, I'll smile and walk through the door. When the stoplight flashes "go!" I'll step out into chaotic life. Making my way through the world wondering how I got so caught up in you. In your happily ever after ideal, the soul-mates, the one, the only and forever. And with that thought, in a swirl of a skirt, I turn a corner and hide the tears that come faster because I don't want you to see.

In this mad hustle and bustle, everything's pressing in around me. People moving so fast, and I feel like I'm stuck going backwards. My head's explosive, and my mouth refuses work. Worried about flooding the universe, I go to the ocean. Leaning over the rail of the bridge, I let my tears fall into its vast saltiness.

It seems the world is in love when you aren't. All the songs are love songs and all the movies romances that end with a forever kiss. It's an unfinished puzzle, and I think you stole the last piece. My galaxy is a scattered mess! Torn photos, broken frames, clothing ripped and scattered.

Everything seemed fine for so long. Then a spark went off in my head. A thought that came from nowhere and everywhere. "Is this what I want?" Eyes going wide in the darkness of my bed. "Is it what you want?"

And just like that —Flash!— everything fell apart. Shattered under our feet and knocked us down. I went away because I couldn't take the sadness anymore. You stayed and blamed me.

Standing on the edge of the pier, my tears have finally run out leaving me empty. I wonder if raisins cried away all their tears, if that's what makes them shriveled and small. Wooden planks on the sea aren't as comfortable as a warm bed. But pin-prick stars fill the sky, flickering and blinking so far away. Blinking for every change that's happening for every moment of every day in every life. If nothing else, the stars care. Gazing up at them, I know that hundreds of their infinite selves are blinking for the changes waiting for me tomorrow. My lips stretch into a smile, and in that moment, a shooting star flares and dies before my eyes.

I made a wish. I closed my eyes, clasped my hands over my heart, frowned slightly then whispered my wish to the sky.

blink

Erin Murphey has always dreamed of being a writer and has found her greatest inspirations in what she observes in the lives of her peers and her experiences growing up in Nome, Alaska.

blink

Tell Me Something Beautiful

I was never the only woman in love with Julio—even his little dog used to wait outside his door for him, growl at me when I went to his house, and cuddle up to him protectively. He'd laugh, and say, "Perra loca!"

Now, it's August in Madrid, and things are bad. Old people are dying in Paris, and my skin breaks out into a red rash when I'm outside. I go to the hospital to see what I should do and they ask me three questions: "What do you spend your afternoons doing?" "Do you see Spanish people outside playing sports in the afternoons?" "Are you serious?"

I answered them "Playing tennis," "Well, the people I play tennis with," and upon the last question I just nodded, said "Gracias," and left.

So now instead of playing tennis every afternoon, I go home and eat lunch and take a siesta like normal Spanish people do. Except all the normal Spanish people are on vacation in August, in Galicia eating seafood, in Valencia eating paella, or in their pueblo eating ham. The only people left in Madrid are the gypsies, burning English tourists, and Mercedes and I, contracted by the bilingual school for which we both work to redesign the teenager's curriculum.

We are practically teenagers ourselves, Mercedes and I, and of course spent every last cent of our monthly salary as we earned it the past year. August snuck up on us, finding us broke and with no money for a vacation. We are lucky to have work. Otherwise, we would have to collect unemployment and that would make us feel like gypsies, whom, despite the fact that we are intimately sharing an entire European capital with this month, we both hate.

Mercedes sees me and my mala cara that I've been wearing since Julio left me, and asks me what's wrong. "I can't sleep," I say, "And when I do, I have bad dreams."

"What kind of bad dreams?" She asks. I don't want to tell her. They're dreams in which Julio leaves me over and over again. He's sitting on his bed and saying, "My life has changed."

The problem is that since Julio's life changed mine stopped changing. Every day is the same—long and numb. The food all tastes like eggs cooked in too much olive oil, the drinks all taste like city tap water, the nights all look like crowds of people, and the music all sounds like flamenco— sad, but too fast for a gringa to keep up with. And every morning when the sun comes up and another day begins, it feels like the last one never ended.

Mercedes suggests that I keep a dream journal. "Write it in Spanish," she says.

After work, I go to the Chino store and buy a little green notebook. At the top of every page I write "Hoy he soñado con Julio." Today I dreamt of Julio.

The next weekend, Mercedes and I take the bus to Granada. We see the Alhambra, drink Arabic tea, and do our best not to get robbed. I write in my dream journal:

Los abuelos de Julio son de Andalucía y todo el mundo

aquí se parece a el. El hombre que trabaja en el hostal tiene sus ojos pequeñitos, los niños en la calle jugando al fútbol se mueven como el, y todos los Árabes vendiendo joyas tienen la piel del mismo color que el.

Mercedes gets irritated that I've brought my mala cara on vacation to Granada and back to Madrid and forces me to go out with her friends.

"I shouldn't drink," I tell her. "The doctor said I should only drink hydrating liquids. Not even coke. Just water, juice, and Aquarius."

She rolls her eyes and gives me twenty minutes to get ready. She's right—I can go out, and I won't get sick. My skin breaks out into a rash, but the heat itself doesn't bother me-- I can't even feel it.

Her friends bring rum over and we botellón and then go to a hip-hop club. It's empty, being August, and it's just us and the tall, very dark African men who sell pirated CDs on blankets on the street.

I dance with the first man I see. He asks my name, and I pretend I don't speak Spanish. Then English, German and French. I dance with him for a long time. Then one of Mercedes' friends, Javier comes over and starts talking to me. "Cuéntame algo bonito."

Tell me something beautiful. I roll my eyes and speak to him in English, "You Spanish men are all the same."

"Come on, tell me something beautiful."

I try to change the way the conversation is going. I gesture over to Mercedes and the others.

"Mercedes is drunk. And crazy. She doesn't even have

any reason to be so happy."

"Please." He stops smiling. "Please tell me something beautiful."

"Look at her. I've been living with her for over a year. She finds some guy at every club. He's probably coming home with us tonight. She'll never change."

He goes to the bar and gets us glasses of water. I drink mine in one long sip, tipping my head back and closing my eyes. When I open them back up, Javier has his hand on my waist. It's as if my whole body was asleep and he's woken up the part he's touching. He's looking directly into my eyes in the way that all Spanish men do, whether they're nine years old and asking you if they can go to the bathroom, or ninety years old and giving you directions. They look at you as if you're the Mediterranean and they've dropped their keys in, but are sure that if they look hard enough, they'll find them.

"Come on, tell me something beautiful," his eyes are saying. Then the lights come on, and he is exposed and personalized, sweaty and bald beyond his twenty-five years.

"My life has changed." I want to say it, just to see what it feels like, but I don't.

We can't get a taxi, so we walk back up the Calle Alcalá to our apartment.

It's so hot out it's like an oven. You can feel the air pulsing, and everybody is out on the street, desperate for some relief. Drunken people are walking home and urine runs through the cobblestone in miniature rivers. We are silent. We get to where they have their car parked, and Javier doesn't lean up against it like I expect him to.

"I'm sorry I didn't tell you anything beautiful," I say.

"Everything you told me was beautiful," he says. He gives me the dos besos and gets into the car with the others.

Mercedes and I take the elevator up and walk down the hallway to our rooms. It's morning and the sun is up, already burning through the hole in my persiana, which is the wooden curtain that's supposed to keep out the heat. I know that, as it rises higher and higher in the sky, as morning becomes midday becomes lunchtime, the sun will move through the hole and make its way up my body so that by two o'clock, the sun will beat down on my head.

I pass out in my clothes, so tired that I don't dream of anything, not Mercedes coming in to take my shoes off and cover me with a sheet, nor the ghost hand warming my body.

Annie McGreevy is currently a reluctant English teacher and injured ultimate frisbee player in Madrid, Spain. For those reasons, she is writing more and more everyday.

— Carla Firey —

Retribution

The moonlight streamed through the bedroom windows and illuminated her face. In that instant, I knew it was over. Her dark eyes blazed with fury at my violation. Her body stood rigid and still, stiff with rage. I begged for forgiveness but she refused to hear my pleas.

"I'm sorry," I said. "I'm sorry."

"Stupid," she hissed, her soft voice made harsh with anger. "How did you think I was going to react? Did you think I was just going to sit here and let you do this to me?"

Shadows from the trees outside fell across my body like invisible chains, holding me in place. I stood motionless, arms outstretched in remorse, as she approached.

Regret swept over me like a pounding wave of fear and sadness. I searched for soothing words of apology, but my mind struggled beneath a weight of dread.

"I'm sorry," I repeated.

She did not reply.

Her silk nightgown grazed her slender figure as she walked around the bed, and the scent of her jasmine perfume wafted through the air.

"Please don't do this," I said. "Please." My pleading voice seemed to die in the quiet air. Even the crickets, once audible through the open window, had ceased their chirping songs.

She paused, and in the clarity of the moment I saw the twitch of her finger as she pulled the trigger of her .38 Smith & Wesson.

For the first time in my career as a burglar, I had chosen the wrong house.

Carla Firey lives in Pennsylvania with her husband, two dogs and one cat, where she spends her days writing about crime, punishment and the darker side of the night.

— Donna McClanahan —

Stains

My wife, Regina, could work miracles on my clothes. It seemed she could get the stains out of anything, well, almost. That's where she was going that day, to buy laundry detergent, or so she said, when she was almost killed by a raving maniac, at the three way intersection, under the caution light on South Irvine Road.

I always thought those yellow caution lights were kinda useless. Give me a stop light, a full red stop, with no room for personal judgement. But, a yellow light flashing caution means look around, take your chances; go when you think its safe. I should have paid more attention to that big yellow flashing light, taken its warning, but I have the kind of judgement that gets stuck under the skin like a splinter, and no amount of digging gets rid of it, a constant reminder of my mistakes.

I was building shelves for the Miller's that day, old man Herman and his wife, Penelope. They had a closet filled with nothing but cases of whiskey, in half-pints, and every so often throughout the day, while I was working, one of them would open another bottle. I kept thinking they should buy bigger bottles, cause they kept it up all day. In the afternoon when I was almost finished, Mrs. Miller came in and asked me if I could take her down the road a piece to Robert Johnson's place. Robert was a bootlegger and everybody knew it. I couldn't imagine what she needed, but hey, what's it to me.

She could barely stand up, and I knew she couldn't drive, so I agreed to take her. "Just give me a minute to finish up and I'll be glad to run you down there, " I said. I cleaned up my project, loaded my tools and pulled my truck around to the front, tooted the horn, and low and behold, if that woman didn't come out of the house without a stitch of clothes on, buck naked. She climbed in my truck like it weren't nothing. I looked at her for a minute, couldn't help it, then I said, "Penelope," I figured we had just gone past the formality of that Mrs. Miller business, "Penelope," I said, "Did you know you don't have any clothes on?"

"It's okay," she said, "Herman's not home, just take me down to Robert's house." I figured there was no use trying to reason with her so I pulled out of the driveway and headed on down to Johnson's. It was just a few miles on a country road, what the hell? I have to admit I was amused by the whole episode and for a minute, pictured myself at the lodge Friday night, telling this doozy. I pulled my old clunker down the lane behind Robert's house and Penelope jumped out of the truck.

"Stay put, sugar, I'll be right back," she said. I thought about leaving her there but I have to admit I was curious to see ole Johnson's face when he opened the door. I felt like a prowling cat, waiting for its prey. Penelope knocked and banged on the door several times, but he wasn't home, or wasn't coming to the door if he was. Robert's was like a shanty town all by itself, run down shacks and outbuildings riddled the place. I figured a guy like Robert Johnson had a lookout, somewhere, to see who was coming, before they got there. His judgement must have been better than mine.

Penelope came trottin' back to the truck and plopped herself up in the seat, a little closer to me this time. I was beginning to think maybe I was the prey, I could just feel Robert's old cat eyes looking out some hidden peep hole, having his own gut wrencher. I pulled at my collar for air, then rolled down my window and peeled out. I couldn't get back to the Miller's house fast enough as the possibilities flashed before me. Sheriff Powell could've been watchin' Robert's place, I hadn't even thought to find out where Herman Miller had actually gone, or if he would be home by the time we got back, or if he was the jealous type, maybe had a gun. Not to mention the neighbors who always seemed to know everybody else's business. I just wanted this whole thing over with, so it could be funny again, but just now it was anything but funny, and I was beginning to get a little scared.

That's when I saw the caution light at the three-way. I had to drive through it on the way to Robert's, but I didn't remember. I didn't remember stopping, looking for traffic, taking my turn. I wondered who had been at that light the first time, had seen me and Penelope. What was I thinking? My wife would've said, what was I thinking with?

I prayed, not something that came natural to me, but I did it anyway. I scanned my mirrors and the roads in all directions and geared down, but had no intention of stopping. I didn't even see the dark blue Buick approaching the intersection from the right until I was half way through my turn. I over-estimated my old half-ton just a bit, crossing the center lane. As we leaned into the turn, almost on two wheels, my ragdoll companion landed on top of me, hair and limbs flailing. The lady in the Buick jerked her steering wheel to get out of my path and blew her horn. I looked over and we locked eyes, just for a second, but long enough. It was my wife, Regina, on her way to buy Tide or bleach or whatever she used to get the stains out of my work clothes and there I was, with a stain no Tide would remove.

Donna McClanahan lives in Estill County, Kentucky where she grooms dogs and writes poetry, fiction and non-fiction. She is married to a District Judge and they have two children and a daughter-in-law.

— David H. Snell —

Nocturnal Omission

Whack! Pain shot through his pores, stinging his left cheek.

How could—? How could the light make my face burn? Then, it dawned on Patrick. Staring down in the sharp glow of the bedside lamp was an apparition, which resembled his girlfriend, Nora. As the haze of peaceful slumber parted like a curtain, Patrick tried again to get a clear take on her face. He blinked, and it looked as if he viewed Nora through the fish-eye on their apartment door. It was that distorted. His whole existence felt distorted.

"What the—?" He tried to rise.

Nora's heart-shaped face contorted into a wedge, her lips frozen in pain. She pushed him back with her clenched fists. She was broad-shouldered, athletic. Even when she was not angry, she was almost as strong as Patrick. "Who's LaShonna?"

"What?" Patrick managed to rub the side of his face.

"LaShonna. You son of a bitch! Who is she?"

"I don't—." He sank once more into a dazed ooze.

"Don't lie to me."

Dimly, Nora's face came into slow focus. She straddled him, leaning forward on her haunches, reigning over the bed they'd shared for 11 months. Her long hair, dye-streaked brown and yellow, hung down like a lioness' mane. High cheek bones crowned her creviced cheeks. The scar from a childhood accident trailed off her wide mouth whose prominent canine teeth added to the leonine effect.

Now fully alert, he zoomed into her talking mouth and half-expected to see blood dripping from her teeth. His blood. "You're busted, Patrick. You woke me up with your twisting and moaning, and then you cried out, 'O-o-h, LaShonna.'"

Nora screwed up her mouth like she had to vomit, but was refusing to give in to the urge. "Give it up, dammit!" She kneed his abdomen until he gasped, forced to look at her through pleading eyes. She eased back to allow him breath.

After gulping in air for almost a minute, Patrick said in a raspy voice, "I swear to you. I don't know what you're talking about. I tell you everything."

"Musta left out a few details."

"I am not cheating on you." He paused, his breath seeking a normal rhythm. "When would I?"

"Oh, don't fall back on that 'we're always together' crap." Nora rolled her eyes, looked around as if to an unseen audience, and brought her head back to zap him with her stare. "Feeling smothered? Is that it?"

"Naw." He reached for her wrists, caught them, and pulled them toward him. But Nora flung herself loose, and flailed Patrick with a barrage of slaps, alternating sides of his face. He defended himself with some success, as her zeal waned.

Finally, Nora swung herself around and off him. She sat on the side of the bed and cried, softly. Patrick put his hand on her shoulder, but she brushed it off.

"I'm going to the john," she said, her back to him. "When I come back out, you be gone."

"But, Nora, it's the middle of the night. Where am I gonna—?"

"Go? How about LaShonna's place?"

"Shit, Nora, for the thousandth time—."

She waved her long hands dismissively through the air and trudged to the bathroom.

Patrick stared straight ahead, his mouth wide-open.

A couple of minutes later, he stood and stretched like he had just ended an exercise routine. He threw on the clothes he'd dropped on the overstuffed chair a few hours before. Maybe, he could wake Benny up…or Walt and crash there a few days. But it was gonna be a cold walk.

Then he remembered. I'll just have to mind-cuddle. Raven hair. Coal-black skin. No complications. No demands. She always comes when I call. She'd been his secret until tonight. Now, he just needed her to keep him warm once more.

Somewhere in that cavernous pleasure dome in his head, LaShonna waited.

David Snell, a retired high school teacher, operates a bed and breakfast with his wife, LaVonna, near Paris, Kentucky. His writing has appeared in *Original Sin: The Seven Deadlies Come Home to Roost*, a short story anthology, *Pegasus*, and *Kudzu*.

— Kathryn Bright Gurkin —

Class Reunion

She woke as he came down the hallway and called out to him "What time is it?" He checked his watch. "Sixteen minutes after two. I told you I'd be late. It took me three hours but the roads were pretty clear. No traffic after we left Myrtle Beach."

"We?"

"Yeah. I left my car in Barclay and rode with Jennings and his wife."

"Why?"

"Well, it seemed like a good idea at the time. Coming back I had second thoughts but it was too late to do anything about it. I picked up my car where I'd left it at an all-night service station near the courthouse and came straight on. Timed it pretty well, I think."

"Who else was there?"

"Well. Jennings and Trinks, of course, and John Barclay and Betty Jo, the Nashes. Serena Pope has turned blond since the last time and Robert Simmons had died. It was pretty boring, for the most part. Same old same old. Do you remember Jeannie Tompkins?"

"Unh."

"She's married and was wearing a diamond as big as the Ritz."

"Don't do that."

"What?"

"Take Scott Fitzgerald's name in vain."

"Oh. Sorry."

While they talked he had taken off his shirt and tie. He disappeared into the bathroom and she dozed, feeling the anxiety of the afternoon drain out of her. After all these years it still amazed her how keyed up she got waiting for him to come back from one of these trips.

"Are you hungry?"

He sat down to take off his shoes. "Nah. We had a big dinner at the beach, lots of seafood. There was a show, some kind of dinner theatre, and a big buffet." His red tie, which he had hung on the back of the dressing table chair, slithered to the floor. He picked it up and hung it over the chair again. She yawned.

He got into bed and began his ritual prelude to making love, small movements of his fingers so tentative, so nearly weightless that had she not been long accustomed to it, she might not have recognized it as an overture to the surprisingly passionate encounters they were still quite capable of.

As she had fattened beyond menopause, he had kept the swimmer's body of his youth. They made love always with the light on, but dimmed. She was amazed that he had never turned away in pity from the livid scar that still streaked upward like a lightning bolt to end between her breasts. That her heart still beat, that her lungs breathed, seemed to her a minor miracle. He took it all for granted, as a lover takes his mate into his arms without criticism or applause. Finally he turned on his left side and slept.

She tossed until she heard the chiming clock strike 4:00, then drifted into shallow sleep from which she woke at 7:00. Through the half-closed bathroom door she could hear the sound of water running. The master bathroom in this house was large, in the style of newer bathrooms with the tub and shower separated and the toilet in its own space with a door, two sinks in a marble counter top, a walk-in closet almost as big as the kitchen in the house before. It could accommodate two persons at a time in semi-privacy with room to spare. She felt luxurious, lying in bed instead of making breakfast as she was perfectly willing to do, but still she did not get up to do it.

He came out of the bathroom already buttoning his collar, putting on his tie. She lay there like a slug, just watching him, indulging her great appetite for visual memories on which her happiness fed in his absence. "Do you want some breakfast? I'll get up. I *will*." She was reaching for her robe, which in the night had fallen to the floor. She no longer took the trouble to wear expensive and impractical nightgowns like the ones she used to wear to charm him—to seduce him. Now she wore whatever was most comfortable or least faded or best covered up the scar. She washed her face, combed her hair and did a quick mouth wash with Listerine.

When she came out of the bathroom still in robe and slippers he was in the kitchen. She could hear the musical beeps of the speaker phone being dialed. With the peculiar muzziness that always plagued her in the early mornings before caffeine she walked into the kitchen just as he began to speak to Lucy. He held up his hand to signal silence.

She had heard the conversation many times before, yet somehow she always managed to block out his wife's unwelcome voice.

"Hi. It's me…. Yeah, I'm on my way now. It took me three hours of driving to find a decent place to sleep. I should be home tonight by 6:00 or 7:00 at the latest." Pause. Squawking sounds like the adults make in animated Peanuts cartoons. "Yeah, love you too. Bye now." He pressed the button to turn off the phone and held her, briefly, hard. Then, without looking back, without even the usual small suitcase in his hand, he left by the kitchen door.

Kathryn Bright Gurkin's poetry, essays, reviews and fiction have appeared widely in both the popular and literary press. She is the author of four books of poetry and one collection of essays.

— Shad Daniel Marsh —

Better or Worse

I remember being at the eye doctor, sitting in that chair with that butterfly thing over my face and him flipping the dials and saying: better or worse, better or worse over and over and he kept flipping those dials and I began to feel it welling up inside of me, first in my chest then in my throat and I tried to keep it down, but you can't, and it all came bursting out in a giant sob and I felt so embarrassed that I tried to make it sound as though I was laughing, but you can't, so all at once I was laughing and bawling, laughing and bawling, and he didn't miss a beat he just kept flipping those dials asking: better or worse better or worse and I pushed the butterfly-machine off my face and ran my hand across my eyes smearing eyeliner and mascara and I try to say something but all that comes out of my mouth is gibberish and he can't even look me in the eyes, he just stares off at his chart projected on the wall and says I think that is an E then kind of laughs because he doesn't know what else to do and I get up from the chair and burst out of his office and see my husband sitting in the waiting room and do a beeline past him and out the door and I am trying to get into the car but it's locked and I don't have the keys so I just start walking, I can hear him coming after me, and then I hear the doctor say from his office door: I hope everything is all right then I do l start to laugh for real, and I can hear Bill behind me now and he says Honey…but I don't give him a chance, get away from me you effing pig, only I don't say effing, and I start walking down the street and its shaded and the sidewalk is uneven which gives me trouble because of my high heels, so I kick them off and leave them there by the roots of maple that has cracked up the sidewalk from underneath, and I blow my nose on some tissues I had in my pocket and clear my eyes; and I know my mascara is running and that I look like a whore and I want to say something to Bill about how he would prefer it if I were one of his whores, but I don't because I don't want to look back and I walk and I walk until the street ends and I cut through someone's backyard that hasn't been mowed in god-knows-how-long and then into a field that has grown up where a building must have been torn down and I walk out into the lot and collapse onto the ground and I sink into the grass and the grass sinks into me and I watch the sky overhead and nothing has ever been so blue and the clouds are breaking apart and the sun is somewhere else and I follow the line of a red brick building up into the sky and stare at the point where the two touch and there is a nest of birds there and I can see them, I can see them I think to myself, then I say it to myself, first in my head then out of my head I can see them I say it over and over until the words are like smoke, and I lay there on my back like I did as a kid except now there are not enough clouds to name, nothing to give a few words to, so I sit up and I can hear the traffic a few blocks away; I can hear the city moving I can feel how it sits on the earth how it carves itself out against the sky I can feel its noise its ache its hunger, I can feel all the things it wants, and I can feel it …and with nothing left to do I start to yell FIRE at the top of my lungs; I yell and yell and I know my voice is swallowed by the neighboring buildings, by the city, by the sky, by the dirt, by all of it, and my ears are empty again except for the sound of my heart and my blood, and I want someone to come, to answer my scream with a scream of their own, but no one comes so I just lay back in the grass and look up at the sky again and nothing has changed, and I try not to think at all, and I am smiling, I am smiling and I'm laughing, but it has nothing to do with laughter, and I clutch a handful of grass in my hand and I rip it out of the ground and then I hear him calling Annie … Annie, but I don't answer him; I just lie back into the grass real still, I try to will myself invisible, try to let my body disintegrate into the earth, and I push hard with all my muscles to disappear, but he is standing there over me, and I open my eyes and look up at him and he is all shaded against the sky and I can't make out any of his features and … and he says to me Annie … Annie I'm sorry.

Shad Daniel Marsh is a native of Buffalo, NY. He currently resides in Asheville, North Carolina, where he is a senior in the Creative Writing Program at UNC Asheville.

A Night in the Country

We lean against the garage wall, hidden in the night, and finish our French fries. I dig my fingers into the cardboard box and pull out the final mess of fries and ketchup and put it in my mouth. Then I lick my fingers clean and wipe my hands down my pants.

"I can't believe you forgot napkins," Grace says. That's not really fair, I think, but don't say anything.

The whole thing is Grace's idea. (Not the fries — actually they were her idea too, but that's not what I'm talking about.) She's the one that knows Robert and she's the one that knows where he keeps his money. She's even the one that came up with our plan. I agreed to it all — she didn't force me or anything — but she's the one that had the idea.

A cold wind blows around the garage. It's Thanksgiving week-end and this is the first real cold spell. The last few leaves flap heavily on the trees and the wind blasts through the narrow and brittle branches. Grace lights a cigarette.

"He can't see the cigarette," she says. Grace has a way of knowing what I'm thinking and then telling me why I'm wrong about it before I even get a chance to say anything. But she's off this time. I'm not thinking about the cigarette but about me and Grace leaving town with that money and moving to Mexico like she explained to me. "You and me on

the beach in fucking Mexico, fucking servants everywhere."
I told her that, if we did it, I would have to leave some
money for my Mom and Grace agreed to that so I said,
Okay I'm in.

* * * *

Grace stands on the front porch and rings the bell
while I stay in the shadows. There's some movement in the
house and then the hall light goes on. Grace has on her
pink lipstick and a short skirt. ("Oh, he'll open the door,"
she told me. "Gracie here knows certain things very well.
He'll open the fucking door.") A curtain moves aside and
then the locks jangle. Guy must have a dozen locks because
it's days before the door finally swings open and Robert
says, "Well, hello darling. What a pleasant —"

I smash him on the head with a crow bar. He doesn't
fall right away, but just kind of stands there for a second
like he's looking for a place to sit down until he finally leans
back a bit and then keeps on leaning back until he collapses
with a thud in his front hall. We step into the house, kick
Robert's legs back inside, and close the door.

Grace says, "He's still breathing. Let's get him into the
kitchen," but I'm thinking about how if we go to Mexico I
won't see my Mom anymore. I can't even write her, Grace
said. This time Grace can see exactly what I'm thinking and
she says, "But think about the money, dammit! The money.
Don't be dumb, pick up his legs."

I pick up his legs and Grace picks up his arms. It isn't
easy to carry him like that, even with the two of us, and
Grace moves Robert's body a bit against her side to get a

better grip. Well, I guess I hit Robert harder than I thought because he's bleeding from his head and the blood is suddenly all over Grace's white jacket. The hallway light seems to glow right on that one spot, a red-pink smear dripping and glistening on the white jacket. It glows at us like some kind of sign ... a neon sign, I think and remember the time I went and drank vodka with my buddies under the bridge and then we went to a bar and then they kicked us out. So we drank in the parking lot after that and Jerry dared me to finish the bottle and the other guys said I was pussy if I didn't. So I tilted my head back and poured that shit down my throat and got through a good half of it before the bottle slipped from my hand and shattered on the ground and then I fell to the ground myself. The guys were laughing but I couldn't understand them and then they went away and left me there. I lay with my spinning head on the asphalt and saw the neon sign from the bar – "Tom's Tavern" – flash every few seconds above me, a huge green sign with an electric hum. It was like there was a fire in my head with each flash and I got the feeling that I had done something very wrong.

But all Grace says about the blood is: "Don't worry about this. I'll deal with this later. This will come right out." She starts again to move him into the kitchen but I just stand there.

Talking to Grace never got me anywhere and so I don't say a thing but just drop Robert's legs on the floor, turn around and get the hell out of there. I jump straight down the front steps onto the lawn. The winter-fall wind is still flying by in the night, tossing the leaves into whirlwinds. I hit the road and start running. I run down that country road in super long strides as the dark woods pass by me on both sides. The cold wind blows straight down my throat.

Jonathan Coony currently lives in Europe where he is an analyst for an international organisation. He enjoys fishing, books on culinary history and pleasant evenings with friends and family.

— Dorette E. Snover —

The Eel

an excerpt from *City of Ladies,* a novel

I n the brothel I take off the burgundy felt hat. Already I feel his black eyes. My hair falls around the shoulders of Antoine's moutarde shirt.

Madame pulls the shutters closed on the sun, the lace halves of the curtain fall together. Her perfume of violets combs the hair off my face. The same hand that held the eel in market. "What is your name, boy?"

"Epi."

"Epi? I see."

She unbuttons my moutarde shirt and my belt. Antoine's pants slide to the wood. She takes my hand and I step away from the clothes of men for the first time in two weeks.

"What makes a fabric desire being a tablecloth, a bedcover or a chemise?" I hold the bed linens against me.

"A fabric doesn't desire, but men do." Madame takes a bucket and tilts it into the steaming copper bathtub, bringing the water level almost to the top.

"Poppy." She hands me a glass of the familiar red liquid.

"Steeped with honey?"

"Sunflower."

"I see." And I do.

"Bees understand." She pulls the docile eel from the bucket. It wraps her wrist. "Come." In the copper bath the garden's heat lifts the roses by the bed. Around Madame's wrist, his eel eyes glisten blackness straight into me.

"So, Epi. Ah yes, the fabric." Madame sits by the tub on a low padded stool. And hands me another glass of the fragrant red liquid.

"Oui, Madame, such things." I drink slowly to stop the spinning.

"In one life a cloth can be a tablecloth, a bedcover, and a chemise. Epi, we are all many beings."
One ribbon-like fin runs along the eel's back.

"I know." Madame's brothel confirms what I feel. The tail of the eel travels her arm, embracing her shoulder. Madame holds its head.

"Being yourself is the most difficult of all."

"Can they live out of water?"

"It's not that they can't survive. But truth impels them to return. Never truly ceasing. Till they find the salt, the sea, their home."

"The City?"

In the blackest round of his eye, a short moment - the eel travels back to the Mediterranean from the Gelise River, his longing averted. How to quench my own longing for home. A different home. His eyes glaze, unblinking.
"Salt." I whisper to the eel.

"But especially, women are like God."

"Maman?" I look in the corners of the shadows. Madame Bouquin unfurls the eel. "Like God." His silvery black skin feels cool and smooth. At the head of the tub Madame unfolds a golden map. "Come, Eleone. This map

blink

once was a table cloth."

Madame holds the map. Her eyes a sadness, her arms veins of blue, her neck embraced with gold, and lips of Gélise summer berries. "Shall I show you? And after your bath, then — yes?"

I nod. A little afraid of my choice. But mine. Maman, I know you are here with me.

She waves to the tub. I raise my leg and lower it in the heat. Sinking into the fabric of water, stirring the surface of my little pond. She touches my shoulder with both hands. "Is the temperature pleasant?" She stirs the water. Touches me. There. Geography she knows. "You cannot breathe of anything except your body opening; going up and up, and then you climb. Over the top of the dam falling into the warm pond of June."

She pours oil onto her hands. Their sound slippery as she rubs them together. My feet have never known these feelings hidden in them. The path unveils a thick scent of rose to the bed. I leave the tub, water running down my back. Lie down without fear.

Madame pulls on my arms and I sit up on the side of the bed. She opens a drawer on the table and pulls out a worn paper. She sighs at the delicacy in her lap.

"I remember." She says. She touches the paper and it crumbles. "Your beautiful Maman."

A red velvet mask feathered with peacock. An attached veil of softness. The eyes of the feathers like the eels. Bright and blinking. The veil of lavender sheer and delicately laced through with fennel and hyssop leaves.

Another heat enters the room. A man in a cape next to the bed. His legs walk towards me, parting the cape in the middle. He throws petals of a rose on the floor near the bed. I cannot look at him. At that pointing at me. I laugh. An eel.

He swoons and his knees buckle. They pick him up, laughing. One, two, maybe three voices near. *You.* He says. *Enfin.* His lips press my cheek and his palms lift me. I climb with him beneath. *Enfin, ma chere.*

I walk up the hill. And down towards the pond. The light grows.
You.
As he mounts, we enter the same breathing. His arms. Thick. And holding.

A field opens in mist, richest and alone, at the top of the earth. Drenched with salt. The sea, heat of the sun, and the bones of the eel.

Forming the crown — he presses against the table. The heat expands. The loaves touch each other. In the oven heat they grow together, leaving scars on the surface when they separate.
I touch his chin, the small hairs.
The oven flames shoot over them.
You.
The light blazes. His back arches. My small world swells. The Gelise. His legs and hands push me into a woman.
Don't leave me.

Afterwards. After the blood. After the tears and the holding, they take him. Pulling away. Me.

You.

I miss the bread dearly, touching the crowns. The searing oven warms my arms, my face. The iron door closes.

"When you leave St. Levain, follow the path. First to Condom. There the two paths cross." Madame brings out a basket. "Tonight —roast him, share him with the man you love. Eleone of St. Levain." She lifts the lid, puts in my map and the eel. He wraps the gold cord. His black eyes glistening. I travel home with him.

As owner of C'est si Bon! Cooking School in Chapel Hill, **Dorette Snover** was hanuted by a 14th century mill in Gascony to write *City of Ladies.* And so she entices her clients — often times, but not always, ladies who are hungry to map their world.

blink

— M. C. Wyatt —
Special Delivery

Rain coated the glass as Kathy peered out the windows looking for her birthday present. She smoothed her black dress over her hips wondering for the fifth time how she looked while fighting the desire to look. Get a grip, she reminded herself, the guy is a professional this is what he does. Professional, even the word raised her body temperature.

Emily, *Miss I Can't Keep a Secret,* hinted her gift was someone or something that would take her to another world, she confided with a wink. An escort, a gigolo, she couldn't believe it? She had joked to Rita she wouldn't mind the services of one. She never knew one existed in the city of New Albany. Would he look like Richard Gere?

Would he take her somewhere? Should she pack a bag? Kathy shoved her toothbrush and deodorant in her purse just in case. Rita being Rita she probably ordered a biker guy or a cowboy. The knock brought her out of her daydream with a thump as her head collided with the window.

A slightly damp deliveryman in a brown uniform holding a clipboard and package greeted her with a cheery smile. This was him? Kathy expected something a little over the top. Someone taller, more muscular, still he was kind of cute. The delivery outfit was kind of kinky, special delivery and all that. He extended the clipboard and package.

Oh, this is too perfect; Kathy smiled slyly before she grabbed her birthday present with both hands and pulled him inside. The lights flickered and went out. How incredible for Cinergy to lend a hand. A strangled plea about not meeting his time table tapered off as Kathy bit his earlobe. Shouldn't he do *something?* Kathy hoped Rita hadn't spent too much on this guy. Pressing him up against the wall Kathy just about managed to wrap one leg around his trim little rear when the lights flickered back on.

Feminine gasps and giggles caught her attention. Standing in the open doorway was Rita, Emily and Sandy. The shocked expressions on their faces let her know that maybe she wasn't dealing with a professional. Nodding in the direction of the delivery guy she mouthed not my birthday present? Rita shook her head and pointed to the package abandoned by the door.

The delivery guy grabbed his clipboard and shoved it at Kathy to sign. Red faced, he jogged to the truck while all four women watched him intently. Laughter filled the air as he zoomed away leaving flying gravel in his wake.

Kathy shot Emily an evil look, causing her to burst out in laughter all over again. Her gift was an airline ticket to Las Vegas. That's what Emily meant when she said a trip to someplace. The someone was the three of them.

As for the slightly mussed delivery guy, there was always internet shopping, Kathy mused.

M. C. Wyatt is a writer living in Clay City, Indiana.

blink

— S.K. Rogers —

In a Wink of an Eye

Her life changed with a wink of his eye.

Oh, it took perhaps five minutes for the full significance of that wink to sink in. But there it was—Alison had crossed her Rubicon, and that casual, deliberate droop of Michael's right eyelid had caused the scales to fall from her eyes.

Michael was her significant other. She never liked the phrase; it seemed pretentious. But "boyfriend" sounded sophomoric for people already in their thirties and partner just didn't feel quite right. Usually, she introduced him with "This is Michael." Simple and to the point. Although if she didn't do it quick enough, he was apt to charge in with "Hi, I'm Alison's boyfriend," which she found discomfiting.

They had been seeing each other for five years, living together for three. They lived out in the suburb, in a house Michael had bought, saying that it was a good investment even if they weren't going to stay there forever. Alison had been dubious about the location. But it was a reasonable commuting compromise for work and he said, it wasn't forever. Alison would rather be nibbled to death by ducks than live in the bland confines of Forest Glen Road forever, with it too-big houses on too small lots and absolute lack of either forests or glens.

Michael occasionally made vague noises about marriage, but more in the vein of a business proposal than a romantic yearning to pledge themselves. "It would be cheaper if I was on your health insurance," he would point out. Alison wasn't sure that was a good enough reason to marry, but then she didn't know what would be.

Tonight they had been visiting a mutual friend, Heather. It used to be Heather and Scott, and it used to be the two couples would go to the occasional baseball game or dinner at the Olive Garden, but now Heather and Scott were divorced. Heather had been the one to move, leaving their semi-luxurious houses two blocks away on Forest Glen Circle to rent a one-bedroom apartment in the city.

Heather's new place was in a three story brick building in a mixed commercial-residential neighborhood. The bottom floor held a cute little French Bistro called Pierre's, a used bookshop, and a thrift store. This struck Alison as perfect; if you were out of food or books or clothes you could just amble downstairs. The apartment itself had triple windows and original woodwork and oodles of character, even if the refrigerator was old enough to be humpy in shape.

Heather had daringly painted the living room in different colors on each wall: terra cotta, sapphire, marigold, deep red. Alison loved it, although she could tell Michael thought it was just weird.

Dinner was pasta with pears and leeks in Gorgonzola sauce. They chatted and laughed at the antics of Heather's cats, George and Ophelia. Alison had a perfectly delightful time. She thought Michael was enjoying himself too, but suspected that he would have been happier if they were still going to ball games with Scott.

They were on their way home when Michael glanced over at her in the passenger seat of the SUV and said, "Poor Heather. I bet you're glad you have me, huh?' And then came the Wink.

Alison knew instantly that something wad jarringly wrong. She gazed out the window at the passing city scene. People spilled out of a café, laughing and vital. Punk rockers and sophisticates and artsy types all ages and races mixed casually on the sidewalk. Inside a coffee bar, pools of lamplight illuminated people writing and reading, chatting intimately across marble-topped tables.

"I mean, that pokey little apartment! Cats!" His revealing, smug voice caused a wave of disbelief to pass over her.

Did he really find a suburban split-level preferable to the charm and character of Heather's vintage apartment? Well, maybe, Michael was born and raised in the "burbs." But how could he think she thought it better? Didn't he remember that she had been he one who wanted to look at the city condos?

And what was wrong with cats? They were funny, affectionate companions. They didn't leave the cap off the toothpaste and the toilet seat up, either! They didn't look a the dinner you had spent two hours preparing, using the latest issue of *Bon Appetit* and say, "This looks … interesting."

That wink. His tone. Did he think she *needed* him, like some pathetic wimp who obsessed over those "you're more likely to be hit by lightning than find a man" stories in *Cosmo*? She earned her own money, was her own person, and in this relationship because she thought it was good.

Didn't she?

But how could Michael not *know* all that? How could she have spent the last five years with someone who didn't have a clue as to who she was?

She could tell Heather was genuinely happy, not putting a brave face on finding herself alone. Heather liked her cozy and colorful apartment in its lively, diverse neighborhood; she like living with her undemanding cats. Heather was quite likely relieved to have shed dull, unimaginative Scott. Heather would probably be dating an artist or musician soon. Heather's life rocked.

Staring out the car window, Alison saw a For Rent sign in the upstairs window of a building like Heathers. Her lips moved silently as she memorized the phone number.

She looked at Michael, caught his eye and winked back at him.

S.K. Rogers is a writer living in Wisconsin.

Pass The Towel

At the Whitaker household, we conserve. We are conscientious about turning lights out when we leave rooms. We don't leave water running. We recycle our cans, but before we recycle them, we crush them so that more will fit in the bin. When we built our house, we picked up rocks around the farm and used them to build our fireplace. We mini-vanned, bunk-bedded, and still use the sniff test on our shirts. And at the dinner table, there are never napkins to be found; rather, we use towels.

Now, I don't want to give you the impression that we each have our very own towel. No. That would go against every law of conservation. I also don't want to mislead you into thinking that we at least use a clean towel at every meal. No, no. If finger foods are not involved, then that towel has a lifespan of at least three meals, maybe more depending on the number of mouths and fingers present per setting. No. All of the Whitakers sit around the table and pass the same towel:

Sticky grape jelly fingers? "Pass the towel, please."

Honey coated biscuit lips? "Pass the towel, please."

Laughing so hard that milk flies out of the nose? "Pass the towel, please!"

(Manners are very important.)

I did not realize that towel passing is abnormal until last year. I am a twenty-five year old woman who has been to dinner at many other homes, yet never realized that five humans sharing the same towel at a meal is odd. I just thought everybody broke out paper towels when they had guests. I mean, family is one thing, but who wants to wipe their mouth in the same exact spot as a stranger?

The Keeper of the Towel is always my mother. Somehow, at every meal, the towel ends up beside her. We have given her a hard time about this for most of my existence. It's gotten to the point that we see it down there beside her and, whether we need it or not, we'll say, "Who has the towel?" and look around as if it's a mystery. Then, the four of us laugh and laugh while Mom rolls her eyes, clearly annoyed.

If my mischievous dad spots the towel down there, he employs his stealth nod to get our attention until we're all thinking the same thing, my poor mother completely oblivious. On his cue, in a magnificent chorus, we'll say, "Pass the towel, please" in perfect unison. (I think I can justifiably compare her irritation with us to that of a small dog with 100,000 fleas.)

She usually ends up just launching it in Dad's direction, (which is such a double standard, if you ask me. We can't sing at or put our elbows on the table, but she can heave a bright pink bath towel at my father?!)

Having to dodge flying fabric while having dinner usually leaves him wrecked. He starts laughing so hard that he has to push his chair away from the table. He takes off his glasses with one hand while slapping his leg with the other — my mother's face set in stone. Watching my father riddled with laughter could cripple even the toughest stone-face, and my brother, sister, and I are pounding the table and trying not to snort out our food. My mother will meticulously concentrate on cutting her steak or buttering her corn on the cob, but eventually, she'll break down with a chuckle. She usually looks at each of us, shakes her head, and says, "Y'all are ignert."

I'm honestly not sure how the towel always makes its way back to her. It's like a magnetic force — like a kinship — like she and the towel are one. But I wouldn't want it any other way.

Alecia Whitaker is a creative writer living in New York City. Drawing upon her Kentucky roots, she entertains readers by exaggerating her own life stories, granting quick glimpses into her country upbringing.

blink

— Kathrine Leone Wright —

Near Long Key, Just Today

Say it's June. Been raining thirty-four days straight. Wavelengths and swells and sheets. Even with the best drainage system in the Americas, say the roads are disappearing. The swamp is full.

And lightning. Crazy, frenzied, light after light after light.

Say you've come to believe you belong in the swamp, the jungle, where even the palm trees are transplants. Call it the paradise that it is.

And that she felt like Cinderella that day, long after the prince stopped caressing the arch of a slipperless foot.

At the moment: lines and planes. Certainly it's as simple as this: a pin must line up at the proper angle to complete the chamber, tumble the lock, make the kingdom fall.

Say parallel lines never intersect, even in the easy livin' town. And the door? Never locked. And Cinderella? Gwen. Her name is Gwen.

On the news: "Despite continuous storms, the hurricane center predicts a slower than normal storm season." But it's June. The season's barely begun, hasn't it?

Tourists? Gone. Snowbirds? Also gone. A good thing, with the going, going gone roads.

Say the prince is a retired astronomer. Neck, nerves pinched from the rotation. A blackbody, no light reflecting out.

And the beach, oceanside? Washing away everyday. They spend thousands moving sand around, back to the disappearing shore. Here's paradise: grooming, pest control, forever keeping the jungle at bay.

Say she feels like the tidal lockings: her same split-open self always compelled home.

She sneaks around the back in the rain, instead of walking in through the bar, instead of scooting under the porch to avoid the water. Behind her, the drive-in movie screen looks like a sail driven aground, billowing and buckling, flicking like a firecracker when the lightning detonates.

She jiggles the lock, waiting for its give. Next to her the ocean steals more sand. Though to be sure, the waves leave their sand dollars, jelly fish, seaweed, coins in a collection cup, right near the fishfood machine. Dane opens the door.

Thanks, she says. Her eyebrows rise.
Nobody in the bar. he says. Hungry?
No. I'm going to swim, she says. Want to come?
Tired, he says. He hesitates, touches her hand.
She leaves it, a nanosecond, then pulls away.

They met in paradise. My adventurer on fire, he called Gwen. My Copernicus, she'd say. My Prometheus.

Younger than his daughter, older than her father. Say they loved the worship. Her smooth. Her fire. Her faster than light. His fine lines. His seasoned brain. His oh, so much time in his time.

He'd hoped to retire to Jupiter. Or maybe Midnight Beach. But Gwen saw the place first near Marathon. Signs everywhere: "Grape cats and aleheads all the same" "Easy rider" "Loose slots and women". She brought his dream home.

Five years later something had changed: the tides, the movement of waves, the swampside of the key all stale and buggy every season, not just summer. Built up to it over time.

Heading toward Key West, you might fly through it twenty miles over the forty-five limit. You might call it Smelly Key. StinKEY if you were a bored child in the backseat. Right before: Are we there yet?

Hubble says objects that are far away from us move faster.

So Ares Restaurant, Drive-In and Bar? Not so great now, on Smelly Key. Which is, by the way, okay with Dane. He came here to be away from there.

Gwen didn't work the bar anymore, and the students Dane hired usually weren't kitchen worthy. Not with conch chowder to be made. So Dane had to be here every day, for the locals and just in case somebody stopped in Smelly Key. But say he loved it, every nanosecond.

So Gwen, she'd drive up to Miami everyday. And the clientele at the spa in South Beach was looking up. The sports massage, deep tissue, hard, mean restorative touch just the thing.

The delivery truck pulled into the dirt drive twice a week carrying beautiful lots of heavy cream, hummus and turkey and rye. Fresh cilantro, sage. A bit of the best weed around. The driver staying an extra hour, four, Smelly Key always his last stop. Done with accounting and commuting and breathing mucky sky, Jerry had nowhere to be. Let his daughters run his company after his wife died.

Jerry and Dane, they could say nothing, there at the bar, an hour at a time. Or, hours would go by without a break between their words.

Usually, Gwen would come home, always after eight, nine, dinner eaten by six to keep her weight in check. Dane would wave from the bar. And she would nod, walk through the bar to the house and out to the pool. In paradise, space looks the same no matter which direction you look at it. You always have a swimming suit on under your clothes.

Nice piece of magnolia, that one. Jerry'd say.

Flash of light, Dane would say. Here and gone.

As she dove into the pool, in the rain, in the lightning, she pictured each muscle moving, like she does when she massages a shoulder, thighs. Their angles, their paths to one another, the knots and dents. She imagines pushing all the bad cells into oblivion.

And she doesn't remember. And he doesn't know where, how.

And say, in the morning, on her drive north away from Smelly Key, she'll know what to do.

And when she squints up at the moon, she holds her hand up, closes her finger and thumb together and presses in. Squished, then, like that to a hot, dense point.

Kathrine Leone Wright's work has been published in *New Orleans Review, Organization & the Environment, Weber Studies, Small Spiral Notebook, La Petite Zine, storySouth, Original Sin, Women Behaving Badly*, and elsewhere. Kathrine currently edits the online literary fresco, *Words on Walls*.

blink

— Su Carlson —

Portmanteau

I magine it: it's a cart. Grs-r kärt: suit-able cage to contain ingestions, indigestions, infants; pushed-by-hand, gum-stuck-to-one-wheel, rickety wire shop-drop-and-load. But all of this is just a matter of fill and spill, isn't it? Fill the cart, spill the cart, fill the car, spoil the child. "Gimme, gimme, gimme," and all that. Twenty-three minutes. Allie's new record with toddler in tow. A new record. Things have gotten easier, better. And the rewards — the rewards are simple and sweet: sleep in late Saturday, a pint of raspberry sorbet, the newest *People*. Maybe, just maybe, she'll take a long bath with the entire cast of some sexy show she never stays up late enough to watch. For now, though, she gets the gist of it all from the girls at work. Who lives like that? Like this?

"Can I help you with the cart?" His voice was smooth, sweet, a little short on the up-side. Allie shoves receipt and candy wrappers into the sleeve of her purse. She can't help but see two children: her sticky-faced daughter and a young boy with too-damn-close-to-infant features. His hands widely straddle her daughter in the pull-out seat of the cart.

"Whatcha think, Jessie Baby?" She eyes the caramelized fingers of her daughter and readies a wet wipe as they advance toward the doors. "You trust this driver?" Allie jokes, pulling each of her daughter's fingers through the damp cloth as if polishing silverware. She winks at the young man and he smiles. Thirteen? Fourteen? Can they work here at that age? He must be shy. Aren't all boys at that age?

They navigate through the parking lot, Jessie's excited "go-see-cart, go-see-cart" squealing in the cadence of her mother's footsteps. Allie's fidgeting for her keys and wondering what she could have forgotten to get through it all so quickly. The trunk creaks foul, slow. Air fresheners. They'd breezed through that aisle. Next time, for sure. In the few weeks since the trunk served as closet and toy box, a musty odor crept into the scattered remnants of a too-hasty move into the city. Closer to work, the sitter. She tries to clear some space. A time-saver move. A more-time-with-my-daughter, single-mom move. Worth it for shaving forty or fifty minutes off grocery day? Probably. "Excuse the mess, um… I'm sorry… I didn't get your na-"

When the police arrive she's worried they'll judge. What stupid woman wouldn't notice a bag boy without a uniform, a nametag? She's scared — a scared so new that its newness frightens her more. As if she's watching from the outside, she's stunned that the officers tsk-tsk her when she says for the sixteenth time, "I just turned around for a — ." Goseecart. She's afraid her memory will blur what he looks like or what Jessie is wearing. Has the sorbet melted? She can't shake the cart rolling into her ankle; how the weight of it stung her; how the thing no longer reverberated with her daughter's drumming fists. Goseecart.

Su Carlson earned her MFA at Florida Atlantic University. She currently writes and teaches in South Florida, where she was born and raised.

blink

— Sylvi Temple —

Midnight Hotel Lighting

Consider this. The bed is draped in peach satin, the carpet is soft, the woman available — provocative like midnight hotel lighting. Or perhaps the bed is used, the sheets creased, a thin sun, up early sidles through the blind, seeks out a white skinned man still full of beer. For every minute a million others, time evaporates — melts in the mouth, a moment slips away untethered into memory and somewhere else, on a hot rock, a cold lizard waits ....

I only ever wanted to be a blink in your eye.

She doesn't bear your name and I am unforgiven. So then our only commonality you and I, is an implausible disregard for timely arrivals.

It was the same if I recall, the day of her beginning—:

Now the hand is reaching for the hour, dregs of breakfast coffee, an emptied, un-expectant cup. With no concern for angry students, who might themselves have preferred a slower start, you take out a well thumbed copy of Satre and give yourself an excuse.

The waiter brings the change and repartee, the day has dawned bright and it is easy to forget the rest —

Out of bed long after the alarm, into show off clothing and Jezebel shoes — shining red concoctions, engineered for seduction and a lifetime of corrective surgery. I am due at an audition and my lazy start means trouble once again....

At the table next to yours an unlikely female orders a

second pastry, she fed the first one to the birds.

Word of the feast draws pigeons in large numbers, and you, afraid of birds, suddenly reattached to the Corpus Mundi, look up from your book and see with dusty eyes adjusting to the glare, the bus you needed, move away from the stand.

Just for an instant you regret your life.

But it is with burlesque timing, that the tin machine has shifted its shadow— Beyond it for a single peepshow second, my bare young summer legs, pull into a waiting taxi, with the unforgettable footwear, clinging precariously, over ripe, to an angry foot.

The waiter comes again, this time irritated by the bird lady but you are bewitched and long past caring. The taxi door slams shut, and so it begins:

If only we could ever know.

Me, I settle down deeply into well-polished upholstery and soon am fast asleep again. My body made for midnights, not for mornings, I am unaware that in the busy road, incongruous and vulnerable like a small hen, one red shoe is left abandoned, dropped in the sleepy disarray and speed of my departure.

Sometimes I wonder if the day had been forgotten — skipped on the calendar, would it have been missed…?

It was a second spent away from thought, where a single glance is a slipped stitch and life is freed from context and without reason. The lost shoe appeared to you to be a talisman, a signifier, a clue to your inexistence and if there was a chance to shift in time and space and regain a foothold then surely this was it?

In a caffeine reverie, further fuelled by diesel fumes and ideas of existential devotion — you don't seem to catch a single breath before the bill is paid, the shoe retrieved from certain death, books and papers scooped untidily up and another taxi flagged and issued with orders to follow after mine.

We search for the other shoe, of course, the driver and I, laughing at my impracticality, but it is absurd to think of taking the audition now, half shod and shot through with a nagging anxiety for my continuous mistakes — suddenly I want to vomit.

Overcome by loneliness, I pay the fare and hobble humiliated into the theatre. I have no choice, without a decent job, food and shelter are fast threatening to become a memory.

Stage doors are never glamorous despite their reputation. Badly lit and cold from the persistent draft — where — somehow, born to his vocation, the doorman lurks like a dog in it's kennel, listens in to half truths, spoken with such belief, to lovers and mothers over bad telephone connections, while stage struck Johnnies keep the dream alive with firstly pen and paper, and then the whispering.

Locked in a cubicle in the backstage toilet, I weep so hard my frail body is retching with the effort. Whilst you, the love struck Romeo, like a bad pop lyric, stand in silence listening — unsure of your purpose. Finally declaring simply that you have something important of mine you wish to return and will I please open up the door?

Shocked and unexpectedly ill at ease with what you've done, you laugh, staring, with a nervous myopia at the sight of my reality. But time is already somersaulted, I am twelve again and lost completely to a rush of hiccups. I hope that you have come to steal me away, because I have been waiting and wanting for so long to be found:

Two minutes spent with a stranger in an unwashed toilet is hard to explain to an inquiring angel who needs a father to dream of in the night. Two minutes then nothing else— Once you hoped for something other than complacency to run through your veins now instead you tell the story over one too many Bourbons. Keeping up with the boys.

I thought after the audition you'd wait as we agreed. I thought you'd come one night to see the show but you never did. Eventually I learned to stop thinking.

This second time together feels like revenge—

I sought you out finally, just to tell you she had once existed, to speak about your daughter's death. Only my thoughts are an unruly crowd and really I don't know how to be sad any more.

Silvi Temple is a writer living in England.

blink

Inside

She watched him walk the winding trail with his aluminum stick tapping the ground before him. Oak trees framed his silhouette as he moved with determined grace and purpose. His body leaned forward as he ascended a slow incline. He saw her immediately. "Hullo, there!"

In that brief second of his arrival, she realized a myriad of problems with herself. Her slacks were stained with garden soil and pet hair and he would have thoughts about that. Had she brushed her hair that morning before coming out into the yard? A quick run through with her fingers and she was caught in snags. What would he think? In those sparse seconds, she came to know him as being attached somehow…to the land, a woman, a project of personal proportions. It was one of those realizations that stiffened her response to him, brought her to that sudden awareness of her age, her failings, the spots on her hands and arms and a face as plain as a field daisy. She found herself standing there, arms at her side, flushed because the garden had lost its appeal, wordless. As quickly as he appeared, he stopped in front of her, looked directly into her eyes and smiled without stopping to correct it. It was a small gift that she caught herself appreciating.

"Roan." He said simply, with a nod. When he moved his arm up to brush a piece of soil from his cheek, she saw the movement in its entirety, as if she were also attached to the arm and could feel its movements, the long held bones bending together, the skin with its freckles and moistened sweat, and like the foothills that surrounded them, a rippled length of sinew and muscle flexed to hold its place, until the fleck fell away and she felt like that too… falling, disappearing among the millions of specks upon the ground. Brown and lovely, but lost forever; instead of coming to the place that made her sing inside. She remembered there existed a place where the world fell away. It was a lovely, lovely feeling to bow down to, though it was all done inside of her where no one could see, as if she were part of some secret ritual meant to curl around his bone and know him finally and absolutely, regardless of his permission or sanctions. But then it was as always, her imagination working its magic once again.

Like all the others, he was only just passing through. The trail wound north up to Maine, over two thousand miles if he had begun in Georgia. He would be almost halfway now. She felt her eyes gleaming, her breath filled her chest. He wore his small pack low and slightly empty. A pocket of air bulging at the top, he moved on up the trail as though there were nothing in the pack at all. Had she been able to hike, hers would have been the overfilled pack. The pack that turned hiking boots into concrete blocks. Within seconds, he disappeared again into the trees. The song of a chickadee chirped his finale. Roan was a free man walking past the point that Laney called good manners, because he could, and because she, Laney Mackenzie meant absolutely nothing to him. She searched the trees to see some small movement, anything else of mild importance, a swinging branch, a startled wren, a twig snapping in the silent wood, in hopes there was some last memoir of his passing. But all was still. It made her lonely. Once again. It made her lonely beyond any comprehension.

Kitty Lynn is a fire marshal, animal-rescuer, garden-digger, tree-hugger, bird-watcher, mountain-climber, and holds the record for marathon writer (40 years). She spends her free-time taking English at UNC-CH and hiking the Eno River with Lucky and Bok-Mei. She is currently writing a novel, a short-story collection and a book of poetry.

blink

Cross My Heart and Hope to Die

L ook at me when I talk to you. It's the least you can do. I didn't look away when we first spoke in front of the hotel. When you were an aggregate of odorous coats and bags in an alcoholic slump against the wall. When I handed you what remained of my croissant—most of it, as I was suffering too much to eat.

It started with the slightest irritation—a fine lash trapped just out of view, or a minute speck of sand swimming along the lid channel. Of course I rubbed it, and rather vigorously at that, awaiting the burning pleasure of abrasion as it snuffs out the itch. No amount of kneading provided relief. In fact, the only tangible result of my efforts was a rivulet of tears, fast as blood, flowing freely down my cheeks. Was my shirt soaked through from distress or saline? I cannot remember. Although I do recall the shirt—Dolce & Gabbana from Bergdorf's. It was one of my favorites.

Why do Manhattan hotels insist on those brass revolving doors? What a nuisance, truly. Especially when one is in a hurry to find a sink and mirror. The lavatory is never hard to locate (although I suspect you'd have more trouble than most, for obvious reasons). Adjacent to the restaurant where the power diners roam from table to table, carrying the stock pages and other props.

What a shock to see, instead of my own familiar visage, those weeping sanguine-streaked marbles! And the itching. It was as if a legion of microscopic insects was crawling—

no, burrowing—into the inside of my eyelids. I was nearly overcome with the urge to grind at my face with my fists. Which is how this scar was born.

Lavage, performed with both water and several derivatives of Visine, was completely unsuccessful. All I could do was squeeze my eyes shut and mop up the various fluids dripping from my face. And blink.

At first I thought I was controlling it—that I had decided to contract my lids 180 times per minute, presumably to exorcise what or whomever was residing in my suffering orbs. But not so. Acute benign (indicating non life-threatening—ha!) essential (medical terminology for "I don't know how the hell this happened") blepharospasm was someone else's idea. Mine merely to implement. And, of course, to reject.

Which I have done with the aid of a steady supply of Valium, Klonapin, and Prozac. And also vomiting, mouth lesions, scabs and rashes, chronic swelling, anemia, and what I am told is a rather unpleasant temperament. (You receive the above as free gifts with the purchase of the experimental chemotherapeutic Doxil.)

Would you like to partake in my feast of pills? Try the pink one first. It's the quickest. But if it's the good stuff you're after, I'm afraid you can only enjoy it in injection form. Directly to the orbiculares oculi, where all the action is. No, it's not as painful as it sounds. The cold electric prick is actually somewhat of a relief. A welcome change, if you will, from the unyielding formication in my eye sockets.

As we speak, I am awaiting my next adventure: a radical myectomy during which the skin and underlying muscles of my eyelids will be sliced clean away. The theory being it is difficult to walk when your legs have been cut off. A bit unsightly, I imagine. (You'll pardon my paronomasia.)

Yes, it is tiring. All of it. The biofeedback, the past life regressions, the acupuncture, the diet of herbed black soybeans, pressed Chinese cabbage, and berry kanten, the endless sympathies expressed in the form of casseroles (why is pity so salty?), the apologies as they all look away. You know about that last one.

Miscreations belong in museums or mythology. Or in the traveling carnivals of old. Step inside and view the Incredible Blinking Man and his sidekick—how would you like to be known? Perhaps we can make a living after all. Talk about the blind leading the blind. Although my vision is perfectly uncompromised by my condition. Nothing wrong with the window pane—just can't stop the shutters from flapping open and closed. All the world is a strobe.

Do you mind if I sit for a while? Or are you loathe to be viewed as my companion? You are fortunate (a descriptor seldom chosen by those with your living arrangements, I know) to have those dark goggles as a cloak. As much as the light exacerbates the spasms, I need unobstructed access to my eyelids. Yanking on them has a mollifying (and lash- stripping) effect. Or it used to. It may be simply a compulsion.

It would be nice to rest a moment. To become invisible once again. A self-mutilating, seizure-stricken soul no more, but, alas a quiet mass of rags on a vent, drowning, quite literally, in his tears.

Abbe Greenberg, a writer and professor from Palm Beach County, Florida, is working on a collection of short stories entitled *Haunted* as well as her first novel. She is also Creative Nonfiction Editor for the online literary magazine *Words On Walls.*

— Hugo Roberts —

Bustle in the Bus

A heavy-set man in a dark blue business suit paid hastily for his ticket and ran along the platforms of New York's Port Authority terminal. The motor of the bus was already turned on when he jumped aboard in the nick of time. He took a seat halfway the aisle, not far from me. Instead of being relieved for having caught the bus, he looked worried. I remembered seeing him speaking earnestly to another jumbo-sized man young enough to be his son. They must have had an argument because now they sat a few seats apart.

The brand new bus swiftly left the city and shortly thereafter glided along the highway between New York and Vermont. Outside, wooded areas interrupted the farmland. The grass was green and looked as though somebody just mowed it. It glistered in the weak morning sunshine, still wet with dew.

There were some twenty-five passengers most of them men, some were sleeping. From the back came a constant buzz of two men talking with their faces close together. An elderly couple sat near the front of the bus. The man was small, thin, and gray. The heavily made up woman looked younger. They were carefully groomed; both their clothes were well tailored and fashionable, she was adorned with expensive looking jewelry.

Suddenly the man in the business suit turned around,

looked at the young man a few seats behind him, and asked: "Sir, can you kindly lower the volume of your radio?"

"You can't hear a thing, I have earphones on," said the young man, pushing the earplugs deeper into his ears. He was listening to the Beatles. He wore a white T-shirt and a yellow baseball cap.

A moment later the man in the suit said over his shoulder: "Your radio is still making a lot of noise, turn it down, please!"

"It is a cassette player and it doesn't go any softer," the young man answered.

"I don't care what it is, if you can't get it any softer, you'll have to shut it off. Anyway, it is not allowed to play cassette players, radios and that kind of things in the bus," the man countered.

"Who are you making rules here, a cop or something? This is a free country."

"He's right, look at the sign over there, you're not supposed to do that," another passenger told the young man.

"Who asked you? Mind your own business," the young man snapped.

The man in the suit insisted: "The noise is still bothering me! Shut it off!"

"Okay, Okay!" said the young man, fiddling with the cassette player on his lap. A few minutes later, the man in the suit jumped up and said loudly: "I have already asked you very politely to lower the volume of that thing, you're not listening." His face was red and he breathed heavily.

blink

Some of the passengers looked up, a few of them shifted uneasily in their seats.

"I'm not shutting anything off," the young man yelled. Then, totally ignoring the other, he sank back in his seat and looked out the window.

The men in the back of the bus began whispering. The man in the suit was getting more and more excited.

"Look here," he shouted, "Play that thing softer or shut it off!"

One of the passengers almost inaudibly said "Yeah!" but the others kept watching silently, some of them breathlessly.

"Make me!" the young man nagged.

The older man slowly got on his feet, he was large and bulky like a sumo wrestler, and stalked the young man like a tiger.

"Either you shut that thing off right away or I'll throw it outside," he shouted.

The young man also stood up. He was well over six feet tall and broad shouldered, resembling a heavyweight boxer. Calmly and slowly, he said: "Sit down and shut up, before I throw you outside."

The man planted himself in front of the young man, looked him in the eyes and barked: "Don't you dare threatening me, brat, do you know who you're talking to?"

They stood staring like two tigers measuring each other before an attack. The men in the back stopped talking; it was very quiet in the bus. All passengers were wide-awake and most of them looked up fearfully at the pair.

"I don't know and I don't care who you are. Throw my cassette player outside if you dare," the young man snarled.

Everybody gaped spellbound when the man in the suit grabbed the cassette player while the other held on to it. Seconds later, two heavy bodies whirled through the aisle. One woman began to cry. The men bounced through and fro through the bus, falling on passengers on their way. Somebody yelled: "Driver, stop! Stop the bus!"

The driver parked on the side of the road and made a rush for the combatants. Together with a number of strong men he was able to separate them. Gasping for breath they gazed at each other with eyes full of hatred.   A passenger explained to the driver what had happened. The driver ordered the young man out of the bus for breaking the rules. He left while protesting heavily. Outside he cursed and shook his fist at those in the bus.

The bus continued its trip, but after about a mile, the woman in the seat near the front screamed: "My necklace, somebody stole my necklace."

Some of the passengers helped her to look for it. Her companion even crawled under the seats, came up empty handed, and said: "It's gone. It's stolen, I'm sure." He went up front to tell the driver, who once again parked the bus at the next gas station to call the police.

It was then that the man in the suit looked very worried again, I'm quite sure I heard him mutter, "I'm getting too old for this."

Hugo Roberts was born in Suriname (1942). In Suriname, The Netherlands, the U.S. and Nepal he worked in various occupations. In 2002 he retired as a senior psychologist and started writing in Dutch and English.

— Scarlett Rooney —
The Weigh Station

I never knew white could bring on water, like it did. I never knew salt was a by-product of the ocean.

Crocodiles were part of my days, back porches, sliding screens, mosquitoes, the kind that buzz and the kind that don't. Never leave a small dog near a canal.

You might not see it in the morning.

Be careful to tell your Dad to take the lids off his small liquor bottles because they'll float down the canal, otherwise.

Someone's gonna notice in the morning, and I'll ride my bike early to school. I knew this at eleven. I was wise to the world, but white—

White got away with murder.

I fell in love with white when I first saw the sun turn beyond gold. The bright of excitement, that just between being a girl and a girl who has—

I got my period the month before. In a dressing room. I was ten, and I said to my mom, "I think I must of wet my pants. I feel slick."

"Slick?" she said. "Take off your pants."

I did and there it was, red tricking down my bony legs.

That blinding white.

I saw it first when I put the money down on the stall I'd earned taking care of animals for the summer. She was mine, all mine, and the sun turned white as snow. The sugar sand peaked its best not under the pinks of our famed sunsets but in its white, pure, steam of motion. Hooves trotting along thin alleyways, covered in layers of white. Newly painted fences that housed jumps in them, colored yes, but only more so by the contrast. The turn-out ring. The mile-high sugar sand out in the woods just—

Then.

Bone. Bone white. The trailer, the ropes, the cluck, cluck, clucking as I begged her, my PJ, to come into the warehouse.

"Hoist her up," the vet said. A wide gray cloth covered her belly while a crane jogged her closer to the ceiling. I kneeled on the floor, too shaky to stand.

Her knee all busted up. To the bone. The bone I saw in the ring just an hour back or so.

They say you can never fix a horse's leg after she's down. You've heard the story. The sound of a gun and slow, fading steps away.

"I don't know. Her knee's pretty bad," the vet said.

My hands smashed together, a triangle. "Oh, God, Lord, Please no. I will die, if she doesn't live. Please, just try, just try. I'll do anything."

Silence.

The adults looked at me, every single one of them turned slowly to me, as if they'd forgotten I was on the floor near the small crane. Except my mother, she couldn't. Then.

Crocodiles. One by one. Ferocious, mouth-snapping, agitating, chasing, quick-legged, fast-moving, water-seeking my face, the floor, my heart. Coming out the canals, hunting for it, for me, for water, more of it, wider bodies, rushing streams, capturing it, fetching it up to snow-capped peaks, to reservoirs, to levies, dams.

Have you ever seen the damn of a child's face?

Water, and more water. The thought of death, white-death, body-white, decay. Water until my shirt stained. Water out my nose, on freckly skin, on the top of my baseball cap as it wiped across my face; the cap marked with two initials: PJ. Gaggling arms, tripping legs—at the feet of the vet.

And then.

I like to tell them, I cried me a canal once. Crocodiles came out my eyes so big and long that a short man with a black cap took all night to save my horse.

Scarlett Rooney's work has appeared in *Confrontations: Essays in the Polemics of Narration, Words on Walls,* and elsewhere. A recent graduate of the MFA program at Florida Atlantic University, she is currently at work on *Two Vietnams,* a fiction collection, and *Vietnam in the Twilight-Hour,* a nonfiction work.

blink

— Sharon Bell Buchbinder —
The Poet of Bedlam

He jogs by with his bodyguards, nods, and says, "Hullo, Mrs. B!" in that deep rolling voice that rumbles in my chest. He is not a handsome man. His hair and beard are unruly. He gets bug eyed when he's passionate. A misunderstood genius, he's been accused of treason, fascism and hating Jews. Our government says he's insane.

"Hello, EP! How are you today?" I say.

"Crazy as always!" He laughs and shows his dear, crooked teeth. "How's Mr. B?"

"Crazy, as always!" I smile and wave my hand toward the nearby picnic table where my husband hides under the table on the grounds of the psychiatric hospital.

"Get under here! The Nazis will be bombing soon!"

In his uniform, he used to be movie-star handsome. I was a hormone-crazed sixteen-year-old when he swept me off my feet. I became pregnant before we were married and disappointed my father.

I watch my children playing. My good-looking son beats a tree with a stick. Someday he'll sweep a woman off her feet. My tiny tow-headed daughter sucks her fingers. She's the apple of her father's eye, when he knows who and where he is.

The doctors say my husband has paranoid schizophrenia. He wasn't always odd. Before he went to the war, he was a happy man and a good provider. We had a nice home, a nanny and a maid. Now, it's all I can do to get him to sign the disability checks.

The police responded to a neighbor's call. I was screaming, begging him to stop hitting me. He was drunk, again, and convinced that the child I carried wasn't his. He beat me as if he caught me with a lover. I lost the baby.

The Poet makes another circuit. His steps are dogged by big men and small women in a panting conga line. He's a literary giant. I haven't even graduated from high school. But, we are together at the same place, neither of us free. He stops running and walks over to me.

"How long will Mr. B stay under the table?"

"Until he thinks the Nazis are gone. I'm sorry you have to be here with him. He's insane. You're not. You're a Poet."

EP looks down at me and I'm drawn deep into his eyes. They call to me to join him, stay, don't go. Be mine.

My husband scuttles like a crab under the table, spying on me through the slats. Suddenly, he stands, lifts the picnic table up on his back and thrusts pincer hands at me.

"Traitorous bitch!"

Attendants run and grab him.

As they drag him away, EP puts his arms around me. I hesitate, then lean and, at last, hold him tight. I close my eyes and breathe in his scent. He recites a poem of love and loss to me. And for that moment, when we are all mad, I am one with the Poet and his words.

Sharon Bell Buchbinder, RN, PhD is Professor and Chair, Department of Health Science at Towson University in Towson, Maryland. When not attempting to make students and colleagues laugh, she can be found writing.

blink

— Wilma W. Reitz —

Sweet Baby

She walked past rows of solemn men and women leafing through magazines. They had come to talk about the "C" word. Conception. Softly, she spoke to the white-haired receptionist sitting behind glass. "I believe you have an express mail package for me from Mother's Choice Clinic."

"We do," she whispered back. "It's in the fridge."

A nurse stepped forward and led her toward an examination room. "Do you know where the donor's from?" she asked.

"He lives in Texas."

"A Texan. Tall, dark, and handsome?"

"Yes, he's all that, and he's fathered three bright and healthy children. But I'm worried that it won't work. I'm investing a lot."

"Expensive?" the nurse said, directing her into a patient room.

"More than I can afford. One thousand dollars for the three-dose economy plan. That doesn't include storage, shipping, and handling."

"Wow!" the nurse said as she handed her a skimpy paper gown. "If I'd been born a man, I could take early retirement."

Inside the dressing alcove, she took off her clothes and tried pulling the paper gown around her, tearing it in two places. She looked at herself in the mirror, thinking: what's a little exposed skin around the hips when you're trying to become impregnated by a rank stranger.

She was lying on the table, her ankles dangling over the end, when the doctor knocked twice and stepped inside. His eyes drifted to the holes in the gown.

"How are we doing today?" he said, as he walked to the sink. She tried to find the answer, one that aptly described her apprehension, but before she could get the words out, he turned on the faucet full blast and lathered up. He jerked a paper towel from the holder and wiped his hands dry.

"Great," he said, placing the towel in a receptacle for bio-hazardous waste. "I'm glad to hear that. Being relaxed is half the battle."

He moved about the room, ending up at the foot of the table, where he towered over the most intimate parts of her body. "I'm ready as I'll ever be to deliver the goods. Let's make a baby."

She pulled the gown closer and shut her eyes. She imagined Donor 1354 from Texas. He had brown hair, wore size 42 regular suit, and had German ancestors. In his baby pictures, he looked like anybody's baby, blue eyed with healthy cheeks. She imagined holding him, wrapped in blue flannel and smelling of baby lotion. The baby grew into a little boy, a miniature of the adult Mr. X from Texas.

The doctor's voice broke through. "We're finished."

But she already knew he was finished because she thought she heard the boy say, Mom, where'd you put my homework? Mom, the game starts in twenty minutes.

Mom, do I have to wear this? I love you, Mom.

She opened her eyes. She was alone with fluorescent lights bearing down on her and walls that tilted. Nothing seemed straight, except for the chair. She saw the chair stacked with clothing, anchored by her handbag. Nothing had changed after all.

As she began to dress, the nurse came back.

"Are you all right?"

She slipped on her blouse. "I'm fine."

The nurse ripped a layer of paper off the examining table. "Isn't the doctor wonderful? That's why his success rate is so high. Women respond to a doctor with a warm bedside manner."

"I didn't notice."

"You didn't notice?"

"No, but I was thinking. Have you ever considered providing cloth gowns for your patients? Nice big ones that feel soft and smell sweet. Like a child's favorite blanket."

Wilma W. Reitz lives on Paris Mountain in Greenville, South Carolina. She has completed one novel and her stories appear in Volume III of the SCWW Anthology, *Catfish Stew.*

blink

— Renee Russell —
Break Down Lane

Rounding the curve on the expressway at approximately two in the morning, I saw the car in the break down lane, its hazard lights signallying a frantic message in the darkness. Someone in trouble — or not? This city isn't known for being kind to those committing random acts of kindness. Was this for real or a carjacking or kidnapping waiting to happen?

As I flew past the car doing sixty miles an hour, I tried to see if it looked like a family situation, a woman alone like myself or maybe a single guy. It could be as innocent as some poor working schmuck on his way home. Or a woman suffering a run of bad luck and in need of help before something worse happened to her-incomprehensible. At this time of night I really had no business doing anything other than heading home. A traffic cop would come by eventually, I reasoned.

Conscience gnawing at me five miles down the road, I got off the expressway, looped around and came back drving slowly past the car. No movement within. Hazard lights still flashed. Interior lights still off. And I still couldn't tell whether anyone or no one was in the car.

I cruised on down the expressway listening to the voice of common sense urging me to find the nearest police station, stop in and let them know about the car in the breakdown lane. But the nearest station was miles away from here.

Pulling my cell phone out of my purse, I flipped it open only to find a dead battery. No chance of simply calling for emergency assistance for the unknown situation behind me.

I looped back onto the expressway, cruised up behind the car and stopped.

Still no movement in the car. Pulling my Beretta 9 millimeter and a flashlight from the glove compartment, I eased open my car. The interior light announced to the night that I was a woman alone on the side of the freeway. The voice of common sense told me I should close the car door, move on and send qualified help back.

The musty heat of the Southern night blanketed me as my tennis shoes crunched asphalt and I clenched the gun. My courage began to return as no one jumped out at me. My flashlight beam slashed through the darkness illuminating the car's interior. No one visible, no heads popped up from the seats, no sound except the wind stirring the leaves of a few small tree branches down the hill.

Relieved I approached the car on the passenger side. Suddenly a face materialized in the side window. Staggering backward, heart in my throat, flashlight creating a mad disco dance across the road, the guardrail caught me behind the knees nearly tumbling me over.

Catching my balance, I swung the gun straight at the car prepared to shoot. Barking erupted from the furry face gazing at me with liquid brown eyes illuminated by my flashlight. A Pomeranian scrabbled furiously at the glass thrilled to see me.

Renee Russell is a writer living in Atoka, Tennessee.

blink

— Michael T Anderson —

Missouri

Looking out the window to a swamp maple, faded to the tint of July raspberries, Thom recalls a chemical reaction where the dying leaves change color. There's a form and a function, a science-bound reason that trees drop their leaves in autumn. Maybe the oaks and maples and birches are scared of the winter, and the evergreens are just braver than the rest.

The touch of the round, red velvet Psychic and her clammy fingers jets Thom back into the tiny room. She tells him its chilly because the spirits she has been communicating with are using the heat energy in the old sun porch she's set up in. But it's a fall night, and the three walls of warped colonial glass windows don't exactly make the best for home heating and insulation. Mumbled voices outside the double doors don't seem to bother her.

The Psychic whispers that she's going to talk to Thom's spirit guides. They release a collective breath, meditating, erasing any thought, simply letting go. The Space Thom's brain waves occupy opens out into darkness. Ideas race across — shooting stars dart by the corner of the Space inside his eyelids, pushed away just as quickly, flickers of words or songs or flashes from pictures, gone instantly. Tingles, electric prickles race across Thom's head. Energies mingle, not on his scalp or through his hair, but there, somehow. Thom figures his head must be glowing.

I can feel you.

"You have a big mind." The Psychic focuses on Thom's eyes as he looks up at her, chubby fingers still around Thom's slim artist hands. She hooks a grin, refocusing on nothing at all, somewhere across the dark porch. Knotty oak trees and turning leaves scratch at the brittle air outside. "Missouri, the 'Show Me State'. You're visual. Show me."

Am I going to go to Missouri?

Thom didn't know Missouri was the 'Show Me State'. He'd never even seen the Missouri state flag. The Psychic waited for Thom to process her clever communiqué. Psychics shouldn't try to be witty. She went on about needing tangibles and watching *Discovery Channel* too much after Thom stared at her too long.

Maybe she's the real thing. Creepy.

The Psychic shook out her hands before she wedged back into her shaggy chair. The Shaker coffee table between them held a bag of bone runes, a couple of decks of cards, and some random crystals that could've been from his little brother's fourth grade rock collection. She asks Thom to fish around in the pile of runes and pull some out. The stones click and rattle before he drops four in front of her; static pops sparking on the wood tabletop. Maybe they should play *Scrabble* instead.

"Bold, very forward." The Psychic rearranges the runes into some form of an ancient sentence with her purple fingernails. Thom expects to hear that he'll meet a dark man in a dark alley on a dark night and it'll cost him twenty bucks for the reading, plus tip, thankyoupleasedrivethrogh.

"You can see. You see more than you think you can. Most people see something in the corner of their eye and ignore it. You can see it, and you want to find it, know what it is, learn its name."

I wonder if she knows about when I took apart my BB gun to see how it worked....

She talks some more about his need for visual evidence and how he craves the finding. So far she's on the right track.

She must know my mother.

Thom tells her about the ghosts. Some weird stuff, sorry — anomalies — like the chair at his best friend's house that rocked on its own, or the kid sitting on the foot of his brother's bed at the cottage on Leete's Island who disappeared before Thom could say hello. On the last rune, she flips it over and curtly says that Thom worries about being poor. The Psychic leans back, one of those self-satisfaction moves like when you get a question right when you're playing *Trivial Pursuit*, not a pink entertainment question, but one of the green science or the blue history ones.

Later, as Thom is lying in the hundred-eighty square feet of dark bedroom, pulling muscles in his eyes trying to 'see', his cat yowls in the hallway. She might be warning him, or keeping something at bay, or just plain scared. Thom cracks the door. Honey eyes flash at Thom before she slinks off to get a snack or to find a nest in a pile of dirty laundry. He doesn't see anything in the hallway, but Thom looks over his shoulder before closing the door and wonders what he would say to a ghost.

Michael T. Anderson resides in Connecticut. His writing and photography has been published in *The Helix and All Hands* magazine. Michael is also an award-winning videographer and video editor.

Stopped

She's only seven but she knows when trouble is coming. The man marches toward the car though his left leg can't keep up with his right. She feels her mother's panic flood the car. Window rolled down, rain invading; the man wears his dark glasses in the night.

"I slowed down." Her mother's voice is not the one she uses for the grocery clerk, gas attendant, rug cleaner. "I didn't realize you wanted me to pull over."

"Important to respect the folks out here." His ragged fingernails clutch at the window.

She's only seven, but she can count the dark, wet curls sticking to his forehead. She squeezes her legs together so she won't pee her pants.

"I didn't mean to do anything wrong." Her mother seems too small behind the wheel; her words are smaller still.

"You saw the sign, didn't you? People just don't mind the rules now-a-days. Don't appreciate much. That your daughter there?"

Her mother pulls her scarf up to her red lips. "Really, I thought you just wanted me to slow down," her mother says again like she's a little girl, too.

She's only seven, but she wants to bite his veined hand, scratch his eyes with her too small nails, kick him out of their lives with her patent leather shoes.

The man hugs his red flag and searches the night for a judgment. "OK, guess I'll let you go."

She watches her mother's hands flutter in her lap and hears her knees jangle against the car keys.

"Next time, you stop. That's what we're all about."

The car starts to roll. She's only seven, but she calls out—louder than on the schoolyard, louder than when she tore a doll's dress by accident, louder than when her mother slaps her.

"You stay away!"

Phyllis Carol Agins' published fiction includes a children's book and two novels. Her most recent short stories appear in *wildriverreview.com, Philly Fiction and Lilith Magazine* (Fall, '06). She divides her time between Philadelphia and France.

— Marjorie Petesch —
What If?

Y ou sit in your car at the red light and think about the gas you're wasting. The wait is long when you're on a side street trying to cross a major highway and you have a mental picture of dollar bills floating off into the polluted air.

Traffic whizzes by. Two lanes going east, two lanes going west, with a perfectly manicured grassy median separating them. This is, after all, affluent suburbia, USA. But where are all these people headed, and why are they in such a hurry?

You notice off to the side of the intersection a trio of small homemade crosses and a brittle, faded bouquet of plastic flowers marking the place where three teenagers died. What's it been — almost a year ago? You vaguely recall the news reports. They turned into the path of an 18-wheeler. How could anyone not see an 18-wheeler?

You drum your fingers on the steering wheel. You need a manicure. Maybe you'll have time next week. You punch buttons on the radio, from the jazz station to the classical station, then back. You flip open your cell phone to check for missed calls.

What if you were to stomp on the gas? Right now. Pull out in front of those cars, trucks, SUVs, all in such a hurry to go … somewhere. There's nothing to stop you. You want to; you know you want to.

Would you feel the impact when vehicles hit you? Or would you be dead before you *felt* anything.

You toy with the idea. All you'd have to do is move your foot off the brake and onto the gas. You compromise. You remove your foot from the brake.

But then you wonder: Would anyone put up a little wooden cross and a bouquet of plastic flowers in your memory?

The light finally turns green. You look both ways and drive sedately across four lanes of traffic.

Marge Petesch is working on her first novel and has written several pieces of short fiction. She and her husband live in Cary, North Carolina. Their Abyssinian cat, Primrose, is their only child still at home.

— T.E. Gaytley —

Bats and Dogs

I held my hands on the wheel, in the last instant where my breath proved my life was not yet gone. The moonlight drenched my skin through the windshield and a wind born in the hot, near desert cooled my angry mind. A dust devil was picking up steam a half mile back, kick started by the rushing break of my passing car. I was leaning back in the plush leather seat, the weight of all my problems drifting away in an unseen cloud of smoke.

The red light overhead and across the intersection flashed, revealing a treacherous road stretched out far beyond the worn out old town, where only three buildings still stood occupied. A desolate view burned in the red glow and then the flashing light blinked out into darkness.

A smashing crash reached my ears along the soft air.

In the gas station one block back, Tom, the attendant who had pointed me toward the Nightwind Hotel a half mile further up the road, dropped his plate of pancakes before the sound reached him. The plate crashed at that same instant when the gunshot's cruel arm reached into the darkened night.

Crossing the street, a stray dog's ears pricked up like his mighty ancestors in a time of canine warfare. The alien explosion distracted his instinctive heart for no time he would remember. In the black sky above, a bat snatched a giant moth in its gaping jaw, losing track of its equilibrium only briefly.

Behind the thin but protective walls of a single wide trailer three blocks over, a fat couple was hosting a makeshift orgy with three old friends from Reno. The gunshot coincided with an orgasm splattering on the face of the contentedly drunken matron of the house.

Garbage cans and empty public mailboxes caught the noise in their metal bellies and let the vibrations dance together until weary.

My destination hotel hovered over hell, balancing on the dirt with delicate clumsiness. In that black instant intersection, two lights were on in adjoining upstairs rooms. Inside, a deal was going down that I was to be a part of. Two men argued with quiet eyes while they awaited my delivery. Impatience and greed had won the day and my mind flashed to the briefcase on the floor next to me.

The red light flashed back on and I hungrily snatched up the view in my rearview mirror. Drenched in red, both soft light and dark liquid, my head lolled as the blood poured into my eye. The last breath rushed out of my chest and as my eyes closed, I heard the passenger side door open with a click.

T.E. Gaytley writes in Hyogo-ken, Japan where he teaches English and enjoys bad karaoke slightly less than good karaoke. It is important to note that teaching English and writing it well are surprisingly unrelated.

blink

Ivar The Boneless

In the Devil's Triangle near downtown Los Angeles, unexplained abductions were notorious. Whispered stories about a gateway to other eras and places proliferated, but the strange magnetic fields and swirling vortexes baffled scientists. After dusk, a mysterious light could change the shape of the sky and those who ventured out never returned.

Broken beer and wine bottles littered the highway. An empty bench failed to attract a bus. A lone man with skin as thick as an armadillo pedaled off on a rusty bicycle. And, a trickle of commuters raced up the freeway ramp to escape the streets.

Last in line, I was trapped by the stoplight. The thousand-bulb marquee of the Viking Motel blinked black. Six-foot iron spikes guarded the pastel painted fortress with a freeway for a backdrop. A metal gate chained like a guillotine hung over the driveway. Only a moat was missing. With daggers and knives decorating the signage, willing guests seemed unlikely.

I thought my eyes had deceived me when I spied a shield and lance wall of spike helmeted warriors. With bare chests like wire brushes and manes befitting lions, they advanced toward me. Swords and sabers dangled from their leather and fur skirts. I recognized Ivar the Boneless, that famous Viking chieftain, from my history books. Unable to walk with his cartilage legs, he rode on a leather-backed shield.

A shower of spears and arrows attacked my metal vehicle. Nimble as goats, the Norsemen catapulted the spiked fence. As they hooted and howled, I squeezed myself onto the floor of the car and hid under a jacket. The pounding of my heart depressed the accelerator, but their mass of muscle halted any movement of the auto. I heard a loud crash and felt the hood split open. With stabbing and slashing and axing, my sedan turned convertible.

A hand yanked my hair and pulled me up. The blade of a spear snipped off the tip of my nose. I feared being skewered like shish kabob, or ground into the asphalt. Or even worse. I could be blood eagled, back split open, bloody broken ribs fashioned into wings, my lungs ripped out, and my wounds sprinkled with salt. Ivar the Boneless had not been known as merciful. But, when our blue eyes locked together, I was spared. With our blonde hair and fair skin, he knew that I carried his genes.

When the marquee blinked bright after that mere second of darkness, I heard pounding on my window and the breaking of glass. Blood dripped on my leather upholstery as a man reached inside for my handbag. Running against a red light would be suicidal, but, my purse, I would not relinquish. Better to rip off his arm and drag his bloody body through the street.

I jackknifed my car into the drive of the Viking Motel to bring Ivar some bones.

Diana Woods lives in Los Angeles and works as a social worker in a mental health hospital.

blink

Another Sad Café

I'm sitting here in a toxic, greasy spoon just off the interstate near Sioux Falls which is where I sometimes stop for a quick indigestion fix on my way to Kansas City. It's the first day of spring but everything smells like rotten peaches and gasoline. I don't notice her at first but when she sits down at the next table over I think I must be seeing things. She looks exactly like the girl I'd dreamed about last night. She's got the same sad, beautiful eyes and she isn't even real. At least not to me she's not. How can she be? Like I just said, she's only a girl in a dream. The same sad girl.

I have no idea what to do about it so I decide to do nothing. At least that's a start. Buys me some time to think things over. Maybe I saw her somewhere before and had the dream about her afterwards. That could happen. But you'd think you'd remember a girl like that. Wild Palomino hair flailing away in the breeze. Wary eyes giving off sparks that dance with the shadows on the wall. Skin tanned, smooth as spun gold. No way she's real. Jesus, what have I been smoking? They must have put something in my coffee. People do that. Muggers, thieves, sodomites. I've heard about shit like that.

She gets up to go. She hasn't even touched her sandwich. Probably noticed me staring holes in her face and thinks I'm a serial killer. I gotta do something fast. So I go take out a pen and go over to her table. "That'll be six ninety-five," I tell her. "But I'll give you a break since you didn't eat your sandwich. You want pie? They've got great pie here." Really laying it on. Big smile.

She's looking at me like I just ran over her cat with a Zamboni. I don't know if she's got a cat but that's how she'd look if she did. She gets up suddenly and flees like I'm a plague of locusts, and doesn't look back. Another dream shattered. But what else can I do? Who'd believe a story like that, finding the girl in your dreams eating half a sandwich in a café by the side of the road in South Dakota? I sure wouldn't.

I run outside to see if I can catch up to her but she's doing ninety in high heels and I doubt I can get a word in after the chest pounding chase she's giving me. Fortunately she's so terror stricken she can't remember where she parked her car, so I tell her, "I've got a truck, you want me to bring it around? We can drive around looking for your car. No charge." She's in full retreat now, pulling off one of her high heels and aiming it at my head.

Ok, I know my approach is a bit unorthodox, but I've got no time to come up with a game plan. Shit like this doesn't happen to an average guy like me every day. And what can I do? I throw up my hands and back off. "Hey," I tell her, "I'm just trying to meet you. I saw you in a dream last night and wanted to say hello."

"Well, how the hell come you didn't say something," she says, lowering her shoe.

"I get that all the time. I must have one of those faces.

Everybody thinks I'm somebody else. You got a name?" She's coming around pretty quick if you ask me but what do I care.

"Uh, yeah, I got a name, but I don't think I should give it out to somebody who'd buy a story like that."

"Suit yourself. Mine's Doris. Like in Doris Day," she purrs, batting her eyes, "the movie star."

And that's how we met. Who says you need to sign up for one of those online dating services to meet people. You just gotta stand up for your own damned self and move your lips.

Unfortunately Doris and I didn't exactly work out. Turns out she's an ex-carnie grifter who trolls the interstates picking up suckers like me and then fleecing them out of their life savings. But that's a whole other story. At least I met somebody. And I don't even own a computer.

Steven M. Newton is a writer living in Santa Fe, New Mexico.

— T. Donovan —

The Ride

The hard rain beat against the window of the Greyhound bus eager to wash away any expectation of comfort. The reflection of the red and green traffic lights taunted each other as they played tag on the surface of the wet, otherwise empty streets. The yellow light was the monkey-in-the-middle of their game.

I pressed my forehead against the cool, clear window and stared at the traffic lights, frisky in their game and not in the least bit affected by the dismal weather. I sat back and lit up a cigarette.

I had arrived early, which guaranteed my claim to the back seat. I was a frequent traveler on this route so I felt entitled to have this area exclusively to myself. As the few other passengers boarded, my view of the traffic lights slipped away. The once clear windows were now obscured with condensation. It was as if the mist from the storm were entering along with the passenger's. Like a troll, I retreated deeper into my seat, not wanting anyone to invade my territory. I was successful…until they showed up.

I watched them make their way towards me. He was tall, wore a black tee shirt over his sculpted chest. She had on a lacey summer dress, which showed more than I had expected to see because of the rain and the coolness in the air. The both had thick black hair — the kind that would shine blue in the right light. They flirted with each other as they made their way down the aisle, skirting by the few people who were seated closer to the front. In a playful tussle, she had come close to burning him with her lit cigarette. He snagged it from her, smiled and took a long drag. Eyes pinned on her; he blew the smoke out of the side of his mouth and kissed her as if no one else existed. As they got closer, they leaned a bit to my side of the bus, clearly saw me hovelled in my little corner and settled into the seat in front of me anyway.

I was annoyed but also intrigued as to why they didn't move to the other side — an expected courtesy when the bus was not full.

They must have been in their mid 20's, a few years older than I was. They spoke with foreign accents and seemed refined, yet displayed an unpretentious charm.

As I wondered about them, he emerged from over his seat and offered me a line of coke. Surprised, yet cordial, I accepted. In clear English he made small talk about the weather, hoping it would clear up. He thought it would soon enough.

Before he could retreat back into his seat, she emerged and said, in a cunning manner "ah, ah, ah…wait", and wiped the remaining drug off the mirror in a delicate swoop. She carefully and methodically brought her soft finger to my lips and rubbed the excess white power onto my gums. We were face to face. I knew he was watching us intently, but I sucked on her finger anyway. It was uncharacteristic for me to be that bold, but somehow I knew it was permitted, which was confirmed by his evocative smile. He placed his lips delicately to hers; his tongue penetrated her mouth. They would let me watch.

The humming of the bus' engine and the blackness of its interior made our world impenetrable. He leaned over luring me closer while she removed her finger from my mouth. He guided my lips to hers. I was a puppet. He gently kissed her neck, and then, with a confidence I was not familiar with, he moved closer to replace her lips. I did not move. I could not move. My whole body began to shake from the sensation of this unfamiliar suggestion: he kissed my lips.

He took his fingers and combed them through my hair. She embraced the two of us in a confirming manner. His warm tongue explored my mouth, his breath mixed with mine.

His eyes, wide open stared deep into my vulnerable soul. I knelt up on my seat a bit more as his fingers left the bulky mess of my hair. They traveled slowly down my back, pulling at my white tee shirt to expose and caress the small of my back, a part of my body I never knew existed until that moment. A moan emerged from the dept of my newly gained passion, yet I was frightened by the thought of being consumed by lust. I finally lost all control. His hand retreated to my face and gently lifted my chin. Looking at me warmly, it was clear he enjoyed the seduction of my innocence. She too smiled and then gently placed a delicate kiss on my lips, the breath still panting from my mouth.

I collapsed back into my seat and in the blink of an eye fell into a state of exhausted bewilderment. I awoke, not knowing if they were still there. And for a second I wondered if they had been there at all. I smiled nonetheless, lit a cigarette and shook my head in humorist disbelief. Slowly, a hand emerged from over the seat in front of me. I smiled, leaned forward a bit and handed him the cigarette. A few seconds later, her hand appeared, giving it back.

T. Donovan's mission is to create art out of situations that others have not noticed, skipped over or simply will not validate. Donovan spends his time between New York, Provincetown and throughout New England.

A Lesson Learned

"Dude, she's hot."

"I know."

"Really, man. She is so hot." My friend Ty was a great guy. He was one of my best friends in life. A person whom I truly trusted. With good reason.

He had married his high school sweetheart after graduating from college and had been faithful to her for the twelve years they had been married. Which may have explained why he was always probing into my love life. Or lack thereof.

"Yeah. I know. Remember. I am the one who went out with her," I said nonchalantly.

"Tracy liked her, too."

"What's not to like." My enthusiasm matched that of a golf announcer during a rain delay.

"So?" Ty asked.

"So," I responded.

"Are you bringing her over on Friday night for the party?"

I reluctantly spoke. "I don't know. I doubt it."

"You're joking. Tell me you're joking. Please tell me this is more of the 'Comedic Styles of Brett Keeley.'" Ty was disappointed. More than I expected. He obviously liked Courtney a lot. Of course, he liked almost all of the females I had gone out with.

"No, I'm not joking. I'm really not going to ask her out again."

"What? Why not? She's hot. You know that, don't you?" He didn't stop there. "She's fun. She's smart. And she's…well…she's hot. Why on earth would you not ask her out again?"

"I don't know. I guess I need more than that." I took a drink of my Dr. Pepper and motioned to the bartender for another. He too seemed put off. Apparently not for the same reason as Ty. Unless he had also seen Courtney.

"Man, I don't know what you're looking for, but if she doesn't have it, you may never find it. Have you ever thought about that?"

"Too often."

"Dude," he became more animated as he spoke. "You have to relax your standards. I mean really. What was wrong with her?"

I turned and looked at him square in the eyes. I paused for effect. I wanted him to realize the depth of the problem. "She can't banter."

"What?" He was truly perplexed.

I repeated. "She can't banter. I need to be with a good banterer. You, of all people, should know that."

He wanted to speak but hesitated, measuring his words carefully.

"Brett," his tone reflected his demeanor which was now much calmer, "she's smart. I've talked to her. I think she can banter." He paused and nodded his head. "Maybe not on our level." He used his index finger to point at me and then himself rapidly to emphasize his belief in our bantering

blink

abilities. "But she has to be able to banter. Have you given her a chance?"

I rolled my eyes, conveying to him that I couldn't believe he would even ask. "Of course I did. She couldn't cut it."

"How do you know?" He was relentless. Apparently, Courtney was the girl he had always dreamt I would end up with. I almost hated to tell him about her failings, fearing he wouldn't recover. But it was the only way to get him to move passed it.

"She wasn't able to keep up with some quality conversation. We had dropped by The Pier to listen to The Groove Agency."

"Dude, they're good. And you're smooth."

"Yes, I'll admit it. They are good. But you're going to be disappointed in her. I don't think she's as smart as you want her to be and you'll realize how I couldn't be with her or anyone like her."

"Really?" He didn't seem convinced.

"I'm tellin' ya, we were talking, having a good time when I brought up change."

"Change?" Ty asked with curiosity.

"Yes. Change. You know most people fear it. But I, on the other hand, embrace it. So much so that I often go into the bank with a couple of fresh twenty dollar bills and ask the tellers to exchange them for a pair of fives, a ten and twenty ones. Or, on a whim, I might even take in a ten dollar bill and ask the tellers to give me five two dollar bills. You know. Things like that."

He opened his mouth but it took awhile for something to come out. "You're serious."

"Yes. And I got nothing in return. Not a single retort, barb, jab or sheepish comment. In fact, she displayed a complete inability to laugh or carry on an intelligent conversation. Like she had no idea what I was talking about. What can I say? She just doesn't have it. Some people do and some people don't. She's definitely a don't." I attempted to take another drink of my Dr. Pepper but found my glass to contain nothing but ice.

Ty just looked at me, not uttering a word. I don't think he could. His face was filled with what seemed like a mix of disappointment and disbelief.

"What?" I prodded.

"That is it? You based all of that on her lack of response to your 'change' diatribe?"

"Yep."

Ty shook his head, as if clearing the cobwebs from his mind. Then he looked at me with probing eyes. He was searching for something. At first, I didn't know what. But suddenly — in less time than it takes to change the channel when a commercial for Fitness Made Easy comes on — I understood. It became abundantly clear. For the first time, I knew why I had so many problems finding the right female. The answer revolved around a simple, yet poignant and undeniable truth. The truth: I am a complete idiot.

Darrin Cates is a writer living in Missouri.

Be Good

Jenna's father drove her to the airport. She was on her way to study in Rome.

"Be good," he said.

Jenna will meet the Italian policeman at the Trevi Fountain. He'll take a picture of her throwing a coin over her shoulder.

"*Be good,*" he said by which her father meant, "*I'm half-Italian—I know those men. You better not find yourself buzzed from a few glasses of red wine, riding in the passenger seat of an Italian man's police car in the middle of the night, driving up some dark road and expect it to end well.*"

Jenna will sit in the policeman's passenger seat. When the police car stops, she will not recognize where they are— somewhere outside the city.

"*Be good,*" as if her father meant to say, "*Don't move into the backseat, even if that's where he keeps champagne, or flowers, or whatever other weapons he's brought. All I ever wanted was pussy. I'm half-Italian. I brought pills and vodka—to slip those panties to the side, just for a second.*"

And he'll be on her, in the backseat: the nice Italian police officer with the stiff black hair and generous smell. Perfumed dress shirts. Smooth dimpled chin and black eyes, greedy eyes. Thin lips that'll suddenly swell when she begins feeling his tongue.

"*Be good,*" by which her father intended to mean, "*I*

don't care if he hands you a copy of his AIDS' test, if he's circled the numbers and words and he's smiling at you with a fistful of rubbers like this should close the deal. There is no deal. Nothing is exchanged—there are no bargains, no gains. You can't expect to turn back now."

And the nice Italian police officer will move his expressive hands, his artist's hands with thin fingers that wander, that grip her shoulders and set her firmly in place; hands that will soon slip and claw with sweat.

"Be good," her father said as if to warn her; *"Don't let yourself become a project that he finishes, a chore that he squares away before he begins another part of his life. I'm part-Italian. I've completed my share of girls, nailed them to the wall, fixed them in place so that I could get my bearings, so that I could find my way and move on to something else. He's lost, we're all lost."*

A drop of Italian sweat will fall onto her cheek. He'll be inside of her and then, a quiet slow-motion moment. Before any emotion matures, before her brain collects the details and meaning arrives on the scene, a flicker eases gently into her mind, a thought passes. Her eyelids close— half a blink.

"Be good," her father had said, *"And don't forget to write."*

They'll fuck and just like the reader who suddenly thinks, I do not need to be reading this, Jenna's eyelids will open and she'll think, as she swallows tongue, she'll think: This does not need to be happening.

But by then the story will be over.

Jason Bellipani lives and writes in New Hampshire. His work has appeared in *The Cream City Review, The Berkeley Fiction Review,* and *Sniper Logic.*

blink

— Janet Hudgins —
Red Light

There isn't a hope, you know. I have no idea where I am. Probably been lost for an hour. Pitch black on the endless prairie, not a house in sight, haven't seen a sign or a side road for miles. Put the high beams on an hour ago; no need to drop them apparently until daylight. I think I was going in the right direction but there's no way to tell now. If I could just see some sign of life where I could pull in and ask questions.

I reach over to the passenger's seat and pick up the hand-drawn map again, turn on the dome light and look for any sign of where I am in relation to a town. But, there's no indication of mileage on this strip, just a straight line. I've been torn between going back or going on for the last fifty miles but my right foot keeps moving me forward as if it were making the decisions. I reason that there must be someone living here or there wouldn't be a road. I'm hungry now and rummage in the glove compartment for anything I can find. Nothing but a few tools and some old gloves for changing tires. Lord, I hope that doesn't happen, a flat tire would be just about the end for me now. I think I'd just sit in the car on the side of the road and cry until morning. And then I noticed a tiny red spot way off in the distance.

It was barely visible, and I really couldn't tell what it was. But, there must be someone there, I thought, as I sat up straight and pushed my foot down on the accelerator. Leaning over the steering wheel and keeping my eyes on the red spot—a light, it had to be a light—I was narrowing the distance between us. It was such a relief to find something at last, whatever it was, and I felt animated. I sped past fields, the crops an unidentified blur, and finally could see that it was indeed a light and it was attached to a building. It was in a window, the only light in the place. I slowed, pulled up in front of the building and wheeled the car around so that the headlights shone on it. It had been a roadside café and motel, but it was empty, probably hadn't been anyone here for a long time. The light was the remains of a neon sign, part of the "V" in what had been VACANCY.

With a book, *Treason,* a narrative history ready to publish, **Janet Hudgins** has been a juror for a history book award and writing contests, written short stories winning a prize from *Creekhouse Gallery* and "best of the year" in "Tickled by Thunder." She has written reviews and community events for local papers. Presently, Hudgins is in her final term in the senior's program in the University of British Columbia's Creative Writing Department.

— Ladianne Mandel —

Blind

Stirring beneath the surface of the skin is a need for return. Those who have risen another day are frequently souls oblivious to the beauty of death. They return to their flesh. To their homes. To their cars. To their jobs. They return, day after day, to this hundred year sickness that drags each of us, like dogs tied to the back bumper, over days and years littered with shards of goals, promises, achievements, and failures.

Elliott was among the sickest. His intentions were wound tightly around his bones and anchored in the heart of his unending desire to go, do, be. It was this drive, this need to excel which blinded him to the rich fabric of his own decay.

Each morning without fail Elliott would rise, release his bladder, eat cereal, drink coffee, release his bowels, shower, shave, and brush his teeth. The moments in which he could begin to reconnect with himself as part of the universal flow were lost in the constant flash of his clock radio.

The dawning of his greatest opportunity came as any other. The alarm clock's scream pierced his slumber, exploding in his ears and propelling his consciousness into waking. As he sat up, Elliott recalled that this was the day on which he was to visit his physician for an annual physical. Such personal maintenance was typically an uninteresting interruption in his otherwise finely tuned schedule. As such, Elliott gave little thought to the appointment other than to strategize about his speedy escape from the medical building, facilitating an on-time arrival at his lunch meeting across town.

The sun gripped the day, heating the pavement and wrenching the last odors out of the two squirrels which had been lying in the middle of the road in various states of detritus since their demise two weeks before. Elliott sped past them in his silver Miata, as he did every morning, his line of sight snagging on their bloodied protrusions. Although he worked daily to ignore the carcasses, their presence pressed on the membrane of his subconscious, barely licking his cognition. According to Elliott, acknowledging weakness, decay or death would be to "focus on the negative, drag himself down, take him away from the things that really matter."

Arriving at the medical plaza, Elliott was pleased to find a convenient parking space available immediately. Right on schedule, he strolled unaware toward the possibility of awakening. Tipping his chin up, Elliott smiled into the atmosphere. How glorious the sun. How clear the blue. How few his challenges.

Upon entering the doctor's office, Elliott was pleased to find the latest issue of *Men's Fitness* on the table in the waiting room, and after only five minutes he was ushered into exam room number two where he donned a hospital gown and settled onto the exam table, happily continuing his light reading.

Dr. Strathmore had known Elliott for fifteen years and

had always enjoyed his visits for their brevity and ease. He expected nothing different as he knocked on the exam room door. Hearing the okay, the doctor entered and closed the door behind him.

It took exactly eighteen minutes for the doctor to complete the exam, three minutes for the nurse to take blood, and another two minutes for Elliott to put his clothes back on before proceeding to the administrator's desk where he paid for his visit on his way out.

Within moments of arriving at his lunch destination, Elliott answered his cell phone to hear Dr. Strathmore's voice. "We're not sure…something we should watch… another appointment in two weeks." The conversation's end was punctuated by the snapping shut of Elliott's phone. After quickly scanning the menu, he looked up to see his colleague arriving at the table for what would be a pleasant meal.

The days between Elliott's initial physical, and the announcement by Dr. Strathmore that he would live only a month or so more, fell from his life and drifted on the breezes that were beginning to wrestle the sun's heat for attention. But Elliott's focus was still squarely on this "business of life" as he liked to call it.

On a cool October morning, he got into his car and began to make his way out of his neighborhood. On this day, Elliott noticed that there was a rabbit lying in the road. He allowed his eyes to probe the motionless wad of battered fur as he drove by. Feeling his stomach tighten, he swallowed hard and forced his thoughts of death away.

After arriving at the office, Elliott reviewed files with his secretary and met with various associates regarding projects in progress. He made it, on time, to a lunch meeting with an old friend.

Chicken salad on toasted white bread. A side order of fruit. A tall glass of sweet tea. Good company. Elliott chatted and smiled, enjoying this ripened friendship more than usual. When he finally glanced at his watch, he found himself startled by the time.

The waitress approached the table. "Dessert, gentlemen?"

"Thanks so much, but I can't stay. I have to go make my funeral arrangements. If I don't hurry, I'll be late for my appointment. That's life, I guess."

Ladianne Mandel is a writer and artist living in Cornelius, North Carolina. She was awarded the *2005 North Carolina Wisteria Prize for Poetry* sponsored by the Paper Journey Press for her poetry collection *Play Them Bones.* The full-length book of poetry was published by The Paper Journey Press, spring 2006.

— Andrea Eaker —

Rebirth

My doctor is about to tell me the cancer is back.

Just before she imparts bad news, she does something with her mouth. I saw it when she first told me about the tumor, and again when she said "malignant" for the first time. I saw it most recently the day we discussed survival rates.

The movement is subtle: you have to watch closely to see the tiny spasm that lowers one corner of her mouth. It's a movement so small it would not disturb dust motes. A ladybug on her lip might not even feel it.

She hasn't done it yet today. But she will. Soon.

I plan what I will say to her: "No, you must be wrong, I've been feeling great!" Or maybe: "But I did the chemo. And I stuck to the diet, everything you said." Or I might try anger: "What do you mean I'm out of remission? You told me…" But taking that direction, my anger finds no outlet. She's only ever told me the truth and the truth is, this should not be a surprise.

I plan what I will say to my husband, my daughter. Dialogue does not crystallize the way it does in hypothetical interactions with my doctor. Instead, these play out silently, at dizzying speed: I wring my hands, blurt words, everyone cries. I feel lonelier for having told them. This will break my life, will become one of the before/after separations that define my past. My father's death. Earning my Master's degree. Cancer the first time. And now, cancer the second time.

It is strange to think this will occur suddenly, that I will have cancer when she speaks the words. When she tells me "Your cancer is back," it will become real. She will create a single pinpoint of time where the balance shifts, when I go from cancer-free to cancerous.

Months ago, a woman getting chemo at the same time told me she wondered when her cancer first formed. She used the word 'born,' saying: "I wonder when it was born?" Her scarf had slipped and I could see a few centimeters of her pale scalp. "I wonder when that single second was. Do you ever think about what you were doing right then?"

I think it happened when my daughter was conceived. In that moment, I think two things were given to me: a new life, and the beginning of my death.

And now it's about to reemerge from the ashes of the chemo. I don't know when it was reborn. I don't even know for sure yet that it has been reborn, because my doctor hasn't actually said the words. I haven't yet seen her mouth twitch. But the premonition of the muscle tic at the corner of her mouth has made my breast tingle: the sensation of something returning after a long absence.

Maybe it was the day my daughter spoke her first word. The day my husband lost his job. One of the rare days I broke the strict diet to have ice cream. Or maybe it was a day indistinguishable from others, some moment when I was preheating the oven or turning on my computer.

My doctor is about to tell me the cancer is back. She

has not yet moved her mouth, but I can feel it coming. A hot curl of nausea in my stomach. A tingle in my breast.

Maybe if I can stop her mouth moving, she won't say it. It won't be real. The tingling will go away, and I will have beaten it because I will not have allowed it to exist.

I close my eyes. Maybe if I blink, I will miss it.

Andrea Eaker works as a research consultant. Her stories have appeared in Mota and Toasted Cheese. She lives in Portland, Oregon.

Pedaling Shadows

Behind me the sun rises over the eastern horizon. Long thin shadows form. My shadow pedals its bike off the edge of the road, sometimes jumping a small bush, or running up the side of a hill. It cannot smell the pine trees or hear the rooster crow, for unlike me, my shadow lives a fleeting life.

I move my legs up and down, up and down. I think about the recent vacation my family took. Two weeks ago we rented a small lakeside cabin. What fun my mother, younger sister, and I had. There wasn't a single argument between them. We were there for three days when Daddy arrived in his dented pale blue pick-up. I knew he couldn't come sooner because of the cement steps he needed to finish for his friend's widow, Fran.

Slowly I begin to ride my bike up the western rim of the valley surrounding my hometown. Pedal. Pedal. Already I feel clammy. This is a frequently traveled route for me, but never on my old two-speed Schwinn bicycle.

My shadow, though always connected, rides in front of me. I will never catch up to it, since my bike slows even more. Pedal. Pedal. . Pedal …. I flip a lever on the handle bar and wait. Sometimes the gears take a while to grind into first.

The August sun, now full in the sky, beats down on me. My shadow grows shorter. I'll probably get a sun burn. Pedal

… Up down … Up down … I take in deep breaths.

I think about last evening when my parents returned from a shopping trip. My mother had bought striped pink fabric for a dress my sister was to wear on her first day in junior high. My sister hated that fabric on sight.

Pedal …. The hill is steeper here. My leg muscles cramp. Normally I would walk a bike up such a slope. This morning, I must keep going.

Last night was the worst fight my mother and sister ever had, all because of that stupid fabric. My sister ran into her room and locked the door. Instantly, Daddy pushed past my mother and shouted, "That's it. I'm out of here." I had never heard him say anything like that before.

Pedal … Pedal … Pedal … My heart pounds—it aches.

After Daddy slammed the front door shut, I stood at the living room window, trembling. Lights played across me as he turned his pick-up around and drove off.

Pedal. All that is left for me to do is pedal. I am five miles out of town; two more to go. Time has allowed my shadow to look more like me.

I turn off the highway onto a graveled road. The next mile winds downhill. I rush past sun dried weeds. There is danger in riding my bike so fast on the loose gravel. One slip and I could fly over the handle bar and plow onto the rough surface. Yet, I pedal, pedal, pedal.

Ahead tall trees offer the first shade and a break from the sun. I carefully work my bike towards it. The road flattens. My shadow leaves.

The shade cools me but my heart continues to ache.

Around midnight last night, my mother stumbled into my room and collapsed on the foot of my bed. One relentless sob after the other came from her. At times the entire bed shook.

At 3:00 A.M. I said to my mother, "I think you need some help. Should I call the hospital?"

"No," she mumbled between sobs. "I need Fran. Get Fran."

I remembered clutching my stomach. Even though Fran was my mother's best friend she didn't have a phone and lived seven miles out of town.

I waited till day-break to leave. I did not even tell my sister I was going.

My shadow, fatter, joins me as I ride to the top of another rise. I grab the stitch in my side. At last, I can see the roof of Fran's house. Only a quarter mile left. Up down. Up down. I have to get to Fran. My mother needs Fran. Pedal, pedal, pedal, pedal. I turn in at the drive, lift my head, and brake to a stop.

In front of Fran's is a dented pale blue pick-up; the driver's door hangs open.

I drop my bike in the dirt. My legs begin to shake. I can barely walk, but my shadow leads the way. I reach out to steady myself and touch the hood of Daddy's pick-up. The metal feels cold.

I go to the back door and knock. The door opens.

I know I will never tell my mother who I found at Fran's; I sense I do not have to.

Teressa Durham writes from northern Idaho where she lives with her husband. In her spare time she works on a novel based around difficulties faced by a couple as they raise their handicapped daughter.

Just a Bang

Jake died in a gas station about 304,128,000 seconds ago, give or take a couple thousand. That equates to about ten years, but I prefer to count the time's passage in seconds. Because that's what it was, really. It wasn't a year, a day, an hour, or even a minute. It was one second. The open and closing of an eye. A heart's single beat. Then suddenly, everything was different. The black sky did not alter its shade. It did not turn from day to night, hot to cold. A car that had been passing kept on its low moan. No, judging by appearances, nothing seemed to have changed. But nothing was really the same.

We had driven the extra ten minutes to avoid the 'Wild Wild West.' That's what we called it. The ghetto. The place you'd end up if you turned 'right at night.' Nobody made that right out of the campus. Nobody, unless they were desperate. There were bad people there. Bad people with mean grins and guns tucked into the low pockets of their jeans. Bad people roamed the hood, they said.

But we didn't turn right, we turned left. And left was nice, with the Rolling Stones humming low from the dashboard. We knew the gas station in the 'Wild West' was closer and would have the rolling papers we needed, but "no, no," I said. "I'm not driving my Z into that place."

So we drove on, Jake with the plastic bag of bud in his sweatshirt pocket, me tapping on my steering wheel, singing about wild horses. The gas station was two towns over. It was in a nice neighborhood. Across the street, a 24-hour diner gleamed yellow next to an old antique shop.

We parked the car and jumped out. I did not bother to lock it. Jake walked a foot ahead of me, about to step up onto the curb. And then he fell. There was a bang, too. Not a BOOM-bang, just a sharp BANG. It sounded like the first firework on the Fourth of July. Just a crack. A snap. Then Jake was on the ground. He had been up and then he was just down; it was as simple as that. He collapsed. His gray hat had fallen off his blonde curls and was lying lonesome on the sidewalk. His sneakers were twisted around each other. His body was hidden beneath his white sweatshirt and his jeans, which were spread out, half over the curb and half over the concrete. A red spot poked its way into the whiteness of his sweatshirt, and it spread outward until it looked as though I had dumped a can of black paint on him.

And it all happened in just one second.

I felt as if I had gotten shot. No pun intended. I genuinely felt like a bullet had ripped through my torso, and that my ribs and lungs had been swallowed up by my stomach. I fell, unwounded, beside my friend, shrieking a noise that could only have come from a dying animal.

Shrieking, shrieking, shrieking. I did not think I would ever get up.

And I would refer to that moment as the one in which my life ended.

It had been a marital dispute. A wife with poor aim.

Her husband ran out of the car. She had waited all of those years to pull out a gun. One shot, and Jake was dead. But those are only details. And details don't really matter all that much in the long run. Details only matter when they are your details.

The Earth did not stop for me that second. It hasn't stopped ever since. I go to work, have a wife and a couple of kids. I take out the garbage two nights a week. I shave my chin every morning and I drop pieces of food from the table on the floor for the dog.

But something has changed, I'm sure of it. I shifted universes in that second. I joined a parallel world, where everything looks the same, except for my body and its seemingly-empty veins and my mind that moves forward but seems to still be caught in a single second like a rug being sunctioned up by a vacuum.

And Jake, well, I still don't know where he went. He's also probably still caught somewhere in that second, wherever it may be.

Sandra Spino is a third-year sociology student at Seton Hall University in New Jersey. *Blink* is her first literary publication outside of Seton Hall. She plans on pursuing fiction writing in the future.

blink

— Cynthia Price Reedy —

I Might Have Stayed at Home

Sky and mountains soared above me and I breathed deeply of the early morning air. A good day to be alive. A good day to be out on my own. I turned slowly, soaking in the beauty of miles of pristine wilderness.

I stopped and stood transfixed, staring at the silhouette on the rocky ledge a good way above my head and to the left. I couldn't believe my luck. A mountain lion rose, stretching his elegant limbs, sinuous, into the mountain air. I had never seen one of the elusive creatures and now, here he was, for a private showing and a perfect photo opportunity. And to find such a treasure on an impulsive, last minute hike. Just think, I might have stayed at home.

Moving slowly, I slipped off my backpack and fumbled around, trying to get out my camera without startling this beautiful beast. Dropping the pack to my feet, I stood barely breathing and snapped photos as fast as the camera would refocus, zooming from shots of his long body to close-ups of head and eyes. Already I was scanning my memory for potential markets for these great shots and basking in fame to come.

Every frame of film used, I stooped to put my camera safely back onto my pack. I looked back up. Damn, the cat was gone. Then I looked higher up, close over my head, and found his yellow-green eyes locked on mine, his muscles extending in a perfect arch, airborne. Just think, I might have stayed at home.

Cynthia Price Reedy is an artist and writer who lives in Estes Park, Colorado, in the Rocky Mountains. She travels at every opportunity, for both painting and writing.

— Jessica Benes —
One Too Many

At 3:34 p.m. I was the eighth cherished child in a family of eleven.

At 3:35, merely one minute later, I went invisible. At least that's what it looked like from the gas station counter, where I dangled my legs and sucked on a red Popsicle. Two employees stared at me, perplexed while three police officers mulled around, talking into radios and saying things like, "We need a 10-20 on the suspects, I mean parents, in a white station wagon heading north on Interstate 5."

Being one too many means several things.

First, you learn to be selfish early, or you'll never get your fair share of anything. Orange juice in the morning becomes an all out war that requires strategic timing and an eagle eye on your oldest sister, who is measuring juice into each glass by the tablespoon.

Second, when your Dad has bought twenty boxes of corn flakes in bulk even though he is the only one that actually likes this cereal, there is no complaining. Everyone must gain a taste for the stuff quickly if you ever want it to go away in your lifetime.

Third, your mom gets creative with how she entertains her kids on road trips. This means endless sing-a-longs and repeated renditions of *Sippin' Cider,* a camp song that has at least thirty-two verses.

You know, it's like being on a constant field trip at the zoo. All chaos and head counts and complete loss of control.

I was four. We were on our way to Yosemite.

Martha, the oldest, was acting like mom, glaring and telling us to hush up. Derek and Jake kept poking me. So I shouted a lot, which didn't help anyone's nerves. John was sleeping in his car seat next to Derek and the rest were playing I-Spy and fighting.

My dad took a shortcut, which added another two hours to the trip, and that's when Mom noticed we were in the red.

"Art!" she said. "We have to stop and get gas."

"Now?" he said.

"It'd be safer to stop now," Mom said and you could tell things would get arctic if he didn't obey.

He sighed. "Fine." He put on his blinker and we pulled into the next Texaco.

"Everyone stays in the car," Mom ordered and climbed out. She wasn't gone long before Jake decided to get out.

"I'm going to get a candy bar," Jake said. "Come on Der."

"We're supposed to stay in the car," Kendra said.

"That obviously doesn't apply to people who have to pee," Martha said. "I'll be right back."

I had to use the bathroom too so I followed Martha.

"Fine, I'll just stay and watch John then," Kendra yelled.

I played with a spinny rack of merchandise until Martha came out. She looked disgusted. "That was awful," she told Jake at the checkout. She looked right through me.

"I told you all to stay in the car!" I heard Mom say as I shut the bathroom door. Martha said something snotty and very fourteenish but I didn't catch it.

The inside of the bathroom was moldy in the corners. Crumbled up papers were piled around the trashcan and the tile was cracked. I did my business and pushed on the door. There was a moment of sheer panic when the latch stuck, but my meager strength saved the situation and I was out.

I didn't see Martha or Jenny or Dad or anyone so I went outside. The station wagon had been right there. Now, it wasn't.

"Uh oh," I whispered.

"Where's your mommy?" someone said behind me. The cashier was standing just inside the door, her foot wedged against the glass, a mingled look of terror and worry on her face. It was obvious she didn't associate with kids, since her voice had adopted a retarded Mickey-like quality and she was on the verge of crouching.

But I didn't care about any of that because I'd just been abandoned. I hunched my shoulders and looked at her with huge eyes. "I think ... they left," I said, and felt my eyes well up.

"Harry, call the police!" she shouted. "Call the police!" She was in such a state of panic that she hadn't noticed the gentleman in uniform who walked up right away and was now talking into his radio while another officer flipped on the lights in a cruiser and pulled onto the road. I was fascinated.

"Are they going to jail?" I asked, wiping my eyes on a sleeve. The big policeman lifted me up and carried me inside on one arm.

"No," he said. "They're just going to find your dad," he said and deposited me on the counter. "What's your name?"

"Lucy," I said.

"Nice to meet you, I'm Bill. What's your mom's name?"

I gave him the names of my parents and he repeated this into his radio.

Two more policemen walked in and talked to Officer Bill. They looked exasperated and gave me sympathetic looks.

"Want a popsicle?" he asked me.

"Yes!" I said, since it was only my most favorite thing in the whole world. He paid for a red one and the cashier asked him if he was going to need a statement. "Because I get off in fifteen minutes but I can stick around for a statement," she said, "if you need me to. I'd be more than happy."

"I'll let you know." The officer said and gave me the popsicle. "I'll be right back," and he went to talk to the other guys again.

It was a whole two hours before my family showed up. "Honey," Mom said, looking awful and red-faced. "I'm so sorry sweetheart. Come here." She pulled me into her

blink

arms. I was so happy to see them that I burst into tears and wrapped my legs around her waist.

"Derek kept poking me and I went invisible and you left me all alone and I talked to strangers," I said and sobbed against her shoulder.

When I clambered back into our car, my siblings provided sympathy and gleeful stories about all the yelling that had gone on during the ride back to the gas station.

So I went invisible for a minute at 3:35 p.m., but then I was real again.

Jessica Benes is a writer living in Fort Collins, Colorado.

blink

— Julie Ann Jones —
*45 Degrees Impossible**

I *won him.*

A prize. The way you win a weekend at the beach or rounds of golf at a swanky country club. Purchased at one of those charity auctions where old gold mixes with new gold to feed our collective guilt by donating then re-purchasing alms for the poor.

"Well, we were going to have Clay put on his tool belt and sing YMCA, but we wanted to make some money not lose it!" The old guard laughed heartily as Mr. Middleton's construction foreman, Clay, a handsomely rugged man of forty-five years, was demoted to red-faced clown—court jester, a shuffling fool.

"Okay, ladies get out your Honey-Do List," Mr. Middleton crooned into the microphone as he introduced the *Handy Man Package.*

Lawyer-turned-developer Mr. Middleton, tonight auctioneer-extraordinaire, had founded this gala some years before to help pay electric bills and buy food for the desperate. He duly noted how decent it was of Clay, year after year, to donate his services.

There under the August gaze of Amless' elite, Clay twisted in the wind as I loosened the knot at the back of my neck in a brief moment of kinship; sickened as the auction continued without qualm, without Mr. Mitchell's consideration for Clay's *problem*—one only recently emerged but on the tips of everyone's tongue.

On the other side of the banquet hall, Mother was positively apoplectic over my low cut blouse, my neck cinched in a red velvet choker. Harangued and battered into attending the affair, her disapproval brought me little pleasure. Already off-kilter from her admonishments to "not do one single thing to embarrass this family," I had unexpectedly bumped into Clay in the buffet line, then spent most of the evening in the bathroom dousing my hot face. How could I have overlooked the obvious? Yet when I got back to the table and scrutinized the program. There he was. Plain as day. Sandwiched between a *Magical Week at the Beach* and the *Blazing Heart Diamond Pendant.*

"Miracle worker with a saw and a hammer," Mr. Middleton extolled from the well. "Last year, Clay's services went for $835."

Unable to mingle as Mother had instructed, I was trapped, welded to the chair where I sat with my brother Mitchell and his wife Gracie at the "forty-something table." Gracie benevolently patted my hand. Clay was installed at the First Presbyterian Church table. Gracing that circle were some of Amless' oldest widows, spinsters and sixty-something divorcees. Bedazzled in their purple dresses and red hats they giggled and laughed like schoolgirls. Their hoots and howls mortified me as they chirped about how much just a little squeeze, a nuzzle, perhaps even a kiss from Clay might cost them.

"Surely, we can out-do last year," Mr. Middleton winked the room a little courage. "Do I hear $835 as an opening bid?" *Silence.* Not even a twitter from the purple ladies

Now I knew beyond a shadow of any Amless doubt, that Mr. Middleton had not meant to put his loyal employee whom he shared an abiding bond, trusted beyond trust, identified, but in a manner of speaking, pitied, into this bind. Patting Mother's hand at a party not too long ago, he had laughed that Clay—a smart man, a brilliant fellow—simply had the misfortune of marrying laterally rather than up and then made the rather unforgivable mistake of divorcing down, way down.

A couple of decades and some years before, Clay had been my brother Mitchell's best friend. At eight, I had whined and whined until Mother made horror-stricken Mitch and compliant Clay act in my backyard tragedies—that summer, Clay died a million deaths playing Romeo to my Juliet. When I was twelve and the "boys" were fifteen, they joined the track team to stay in shape for baseball and basketball and football. Desperate for Clay's attention, I attempted to match their stride, chasing them down dusty streets and thorn-ripping paths imploring them not to run so fast.

That's how I came to set the record for the cross-country run at Amless High School—one that remains unbroken to this day.

"All right then, let's start the bid at $200. This man is walking perfection. Y'all know that. Last year, Mr. Smote, I believe he laid a parquet floor in your foyer. You called it damn near sublime, as I recall"

Unfortunately for Mr. Mitchell, Amless nobility have long memories and not nearly enough time had passed between last year's gala and this year's incident: that moment when Clay's youngest son, born to the village, invited in for a glass of cold water after cutting Miss Minnie's grass on High Street, slipped her diamond ring into his pocket—*the same-said jewelry she planned to be buried in when the good Lord called her home.* Grand Dame of High Street, Miss Minnie's scream was heard round the block and the boy was caught within hours attempting to pawn the ring at the newest eyesore up on the highway.

Mr. Smote slunk back in his chair.

"Does he do yard work?" Somebody snickered from the back of the room.

The facade around my heart developed a fine crack, but Mr. Middleton didn't skip a beat. "Clay can do anything except electrical. Right, Clay? He's so good you never hear him. He's in and out without bothering a soul."

The room shuddered along with me.

Then with a faint wave of the hand, I revealed my cards.

Mr. Middleton ignored my raised hand so I thrust it higher.

Finally, emboldened by the possibility of exacting a punishment twenty-five years in the making, I shouted, "$1,000."

Mr. Middleton dismayed, stammered, "Is there $1,050?" I have to tell you that old man stared a dagger through me. "Going once, going twice, going, going …"

Mother sighed in despair; Gracie pinched my leg and Mitchell stifled a hearty laugh at the sheer naughtiness of it all; Granddaddy, founder and president of the First National Bank of Amless smiled broadly.

"SOLD, to my prodigal daughter, Mary Margaret!" condescended Mr. Middleton, as I have inexplicably referred to my father since babyhood.

Had he actually used the word "sold" in reference to his loyal foreman?

"Mimi, have you gone mad?" Gracie whispered.

Mad? Perhaps.

If I have my way and I usually do, Clay will not clean my gutters or plane the heart-pine floors of Grandfather's ancient house on High Street he deeded to me so I would stop running the globe.

The dimly lit room faded into the past and I am already with him on the bluff where we had once pressed ourselves harder, quicker than ever to reach its forty-five degree summit. Had it been the plot, I could push him right over the cliff into the river and call it suicide. *Who would question me?*

My bid sealed; my revenge purchased with a swipe of plastic; I tossed the *Handy Man Package* in the trash on my way out the door.

A month after the gala, Clay and I lie at sunrise on the greenest July grass bent and bleeding dew onto great-grandmother's knotted quilt.

I read aloud to him the books he buys but has no time to comprehend.

Opening Dostoevsky's *White Nights*, together, we move time forward, backward, east and west, until we reach the end of Lawrence's rainbow and meet Camus' stranger. We sail into Conrad's dark heart until we find Faulkner's Moses. And—after, like sweaty teenage lovers spent but willing to make the effort, we gorge on Hemingway's moveable feast; then, only then, satiated, I feel Clay relax, cross his arms under his head, his face searching the sky, chin up, back straight for the first time in years. I think I see an afternoon thunderhead threaten his blue-grey eyes.

Time flows backwards for both of us and we are sixteen and nineteen, alone on this same spot, standing in the tall grass of the bluff trying to catch our breath after our last, wild up-hill sprint.

Previous. Past. Prior to those few seconds, minutes when I had completely loved him as he panted—his back bent from our last cruel run, his beautiful-sure hands bracing his freckled thighs. Myself, just beginning to know real longing; frightened he will reject me; I resist the crave to stroke a wet ringlet of blond falling over his ear. Together, we studied the wide and muddied river curling a black ribbon below us.

I blink away the tear, willing time to mend the chasm between then and now, but as much as I resolve never to run that road again, I am carried along its tenuous gossamer threads. His voice—dim in the coming dusk; gently, he explains that he has to marry Shelly; he will no longer tread Amless' streets and fields with me. He must be a father—a good one, not like his own. He has responsibilities. He can't run from them.

Afterwards, a slow jog to High Street, a waving off to the village where Shelly and two families await the appropriate decision.

Now, in the present past, Clay willingly does not deny me my revenge. And as dusk steals the final light of a purchased day, I pray the *Loneliness of the Long Distance Runner* into his ear; my words murmur like the river below us. His eyes close in weary repose; years slip away as I stroke his hair.

*from Fyodor Dostoevsky's *A Gentle Creature*

Julie Ann Jones resides in Amless, Alabama where she lives most of the time in her grandfather's house with two spinster aunts who insist on climbing ladders and painting themselves walls. Irish-Catholic trickster. Magician—a keyboard conjurer—tripping easily between whitewashed sheets, hanging unlady-like, ghosts on rusted lines airing dirty laundry. Bandit. She steals signs. Strings words at the Well. No rhyme to her reason. A riddle.

blink

— Pam Calabrese MacLean —

Christmas Piece

My ex-husband is like a four-dollar bra. No support at all. He breezes in around Christmas, gives each kid fifty bucks, a half hour of quality time, makes sure we know what a wonderful life he has somewhere else, and leaves. He's the kids' hero. He's a holiday and I'm every day of the year.

This visit, his wife doesn't understand him. I used to be his wife and I'm not having a problem.

Every year he tells me I was the best. Vows he never fooled around on me. So how come every Christmas I get a card from people I never met? And they can't wait for me to visit. Again!

I never said any of this to him, until this year. I came right out and asked if he was sorry we split up? Would he want this for his life? This being me and the kids more or less full time.

Give up his money and social position? Oh no, he'd just like us to spend more time together. You know, have sex. He says all this looking me right in the eye and I want to ask what he has planned after the first three minutes. He forgets we were married. Forgets I know how long it takes from 'Oh Baby Baby' to afterglow. I don't ask because two of the kids are taking turns being the target in a knife-throwing contest.

He laughs to alert me that the next part is a joke, and says something about being like Santa and only coming once. Wink. Wink. I'm trying to get the knives away from the kids so at first I don't really get the last part. Plus I'm pretty sure I don't know why he thinks it's funny.

Finally, I get him tucked away in the spare room. I brush my teeth. Swallow a couple of stress vitamins. Take my time with a glass of water. I want to be sure he's asleep.

Quicker than you can say 'Surprise Surprise', someone's sleeping in my bed. The time seems right to straighten this out once and for all. If I don't, either I'm going to start feeling like I owe him, or I'm going to do him just so I can get some sleep.

He gives me that look. The one that's supposed to melt glass, licks his lips and says: "Stop talking woman and do something worthwhile with that mouth of yours!"

I sleep with the youngest and manage to get us all out of the house in the morning without waking him.

Next evening I'm home before the kids, and there, in the middle of my kitchen table, sits a beautiful bouquet.

Two dozen long stemmed roses. Red. I think apology. Until I read the card. He uses our pet names from so long ago that for a minute I think, hold on. Who are these people?

His message, "Don't call me at home."

Pam Calabrese MacLean is a Nova Scotia poet and playwright. Her first collection of poems — *Twenty-Four Names For Mother* — was published by The Paper Journey Press in April 2006.

Intersection

I watched in horrified amazement at the spectacle forming in front of my eyes.

From the side street a small faded blue Corolla sporting Bondo embellishments rolled into the intersection, its engine sputtering and wheezing, then dying. I could just hear the faint sounds of the engine grinding as a young woman attempted to restart the car. She looked down at the ignition as calamity raced toward her on Goodyear treads.

Sunlight knifed off the chrome bumper of a shiny black Hummer hurtling toward the intersection as the traffic light turned yellow. The driver watched his rearview mirror as he shaved his already bald head and talked on his cell phone — oblivious.

I placed my hand against the cold plate glass window of the store, an impotent ghost. My hand trembled as I flattened it against the unyielding pane in a fruitless effort to halt the coming catastrophe. Thinking I could intervene, I flew along the front of the store scattering bewildered shoppers and their children from my path, never taking my eyes from the unfolding scene. If I could get outside fast enough I might be able to stop the inevitable.

Heat waves shimmered and danced across the asphalt parking lot as I rushed toward the intersection screaming at the top of my lungs and waving my arms like a crazed maniac. Brakes screamed around me, voices cursed me, but I ignored them in my headlong flight. My only thought was to get to the intersection in time.

Stinging sweat blurred my vision. I could only fall to my knees and pray as the scream of tires against pavement assaulted my ears. I waited, holding my breath, for the sickening cacophony of metal on metal I knew was coming.

The sound I awaited never arrived; there was only my own heart pounding in my head. Dashing the sweat from my eyes, I stood on trembling legs and surveyed the scene with disbelief. The young woman, white knuckled hands gripping the steering wheel, stared with eyes the size of saucers at the chrome bumper kissing her driver's side door. The bald man in the Hummer rested his head against his steering wheel. As I approached the miracle, I saw for the first time the license plate on the front of the young woman's car. *Jesus Is My Co-Pilot.*

Renee Russell is a writer living in Atoka, Tennessee.

blink

About the Editor

Wanda Wade Mukherjee is a writer, wife and mother of three boys Jake, Vik and Kieran. She and husband Subir, a lover of good fiction, met at a party in Laramie, Wyoming where they spent the evening passonately attempting to decipher the "true meaning" behind Hemingway's short story "Indian Camp." *Fifteen years later they've lost neither their passion for lengthy arguments about short stories nor their passion for each other.*

About the Cover

Front cover artist **Domenico Francesco Lio** is a Canadian-born Architect, Industrial & Graphic Designer. He lives and works in New York City with his wife Eileen Sullivan.

The back cover was conceived by **Susan Mountain** author of *blink's* opening story "Jesus Saves."